D1037941

Lifeguards Only Beyond This Point

Lifeguards Only Beyond This Point

MICHAEL FRENCH

PACER BOOKS
A Member of the Putnam Publishing Group
NEW YORK

Published by Pacer Books,
a member of the Putnam Publishing Group
51 Madison Avenue
New York, NY 10010

 Published simultaneously
in Canada by General Publishing Co. Limited, Toronto.
Designed by Al Lichtenberg
Printed in the United States of America
First Printing

Library of Congress Cataloging in Publication Data
French, Michael,
Lifeguards only beyond this point.

Summary: During a summer as lifeguard at an exclusive
resort hotel, ambitious sixteen-year-old Max falls for
wealthy Anabelle and learns something about other people's
limitations and his own.
[1. Summer resorts—Fiction. 2. Summer employment—
Fiction] I. Title.
PZ7.F88905Li 1984 [Fic] 84-7660
ISBN 0-399-21098-9

For my mother and father

Lifeguards Only Beyond This Point

CHAPTER 1

Full moon tonight. Full, sweet, summer moon.

In only his gym shorts and a T-shirt Max could feel the bite of the mountain air. He was happy to be out here, away from the others at the hotel. On the near side of the lake the town glittered in a mosaic of bright and dim lights. Hotel Sherborne rose up, dwarfing the quaint, winding streets of Barnswell and anchored Lake Chicopee's northern end. Max had seen postcards of the night scene in the hotel gift shop, zillions of them, like someone thought the Sherborne was the greatest building since the Taj Mahal.

Max checked his watch again. It was pushing midnight already, long past curfew for hotel help. He didn't care. The town was still awake, the deep, boisterous, half-drunk voices of summer sweeping across the water to intoxicate him. There were parties going on, with girls his age, beautiful girls, and he wished he could be at one of them. But that was fantasy. He would never be invited to a Barnswell party. He would be waiting tables, polishing silver, scrubbing floors for thirteen long weeks. He knew he'd be answering to anyone who had the price of a meal, but maybe something surprising would happen. Maybe he could make it happen.

Work didn't start until tomorrow, but Max could imagine the routine. After serving dinner every night he was supposed to retreat to a dilapidated cabin with a busted water heater and bunk beds as soft as plywood. Though hidden from guests' view, the cluster of cabins for summer help was as much an eyesore as Hotel Sherborne was stately and elegant. Restless tonight, Max had sneaked out and made his way to the lake. Part of him didn't want to go back.

But he knew he would. It was the money. That's why he was in Barnswell. There weren't any decent jobs in his own town, Bradley, just over the mountain, and Max was tired of never having much money. His father, a plumber, didn't have extra to give away. Besides, Max had his own plans—to buy a car and move to California just as soon as he graduated from high school next year. He couldn't wait. Living in a crumbling little town wasn't for him. Though he'd never been farther west than Chicago, where an aunt lived, California seemed like the right place. The sun, the beaches, the parties. *Cal-i-for-nia, here I come* . . .

All he needed was some bucks. The hotel paid low wages, plus room and board, but there was the opportunity of making tips, *good* tips. When Memorial Day weekend started tomorrow, the big spenders were going to roll in from Boston, Philadelphia, New York City. Through wars and depressions, they had been coming to the Sherborne, and Max couldn't see why they would stop now. The hotel had been in the hands of a family named Remington for three generations, run with the dependability and precision of a finely tuned watch. It was several social notches above anything in the neighboring Catskills. Max had been wanting to work at the Sherborne ever since he first heard about it. Waiters had to be sixteen, and back in February, finally, he'd produced his birth certificate, filled out an application, and waited, hoping he'd be notified of the position.

The party noises were beginning to fade. Max picked

himself up reluctantly. Like an unsteady camera, the moon had printed a wobbly replica of the hotel on the water, a four-story Victorian colossus with a red gambrel roof and dormer windows and louvered shutters. Surrounding it on several acres were private cottages camouflaged by towering spruces and pines. The setting was gorgeous, but Max thought it also looked like a prison. So many rules. No fraternizing with hotel guests. No fraternizing with Barnswell residents, even on his time off. No swimming in the lake, at least not on the hotel's private beach. No drinking or smoking on hotel premises. Rules, dumb rules, he thought, just like at school. They made him feel hemmed in. Max cocked his muscular arm and skipped a flat rock across the water—two, three, four, five—until the hotel blurred and dissolved softly in concentric rings.

Two voices suddenly drifted up from below. Max froze under a scraggly pine as his glance jumped to the boy and girl about a hundred yards away. They had parked their car on the road between the hotel and the lake, and now, barefoot and holding hands, were strolling on the sandy apron bordering the lake that everyone called "the beach." Near a lifeguard tower, their grip broke apart and the couple kissed. Then they began to slip out of their clothes. Their heads swung around to make certain they were alone and unobserved. After a moment the girl laughed mischievously and plunged into the water; the moonlight cut a swatch across her small, tight belly.

Max felt his blood jump. His temples pounded like a drum.

"Come on, Hunter!" the girl chided. "Last one in—"

The boy lingered on the beach, glancing around as if unsure they should be there, but finally dashed into the lake.

A glint of the moon reflected on something hanging around the girl's neck as she twisted and rolled in the water. A key, Max decided, a key on a chain. Did it open her heart? Her house? Did it belong to her boyfriend? He stared at the key longingly. He knew if she used it on him it would open his heart to her. Even in the grainy darkness he could tell that she was beautiful, magnificently so—silvery and slender like a mermaid.

"Anabelle," the boy finally cried, splashing alone toward shore. "Get your butt out. It's time to get home."

"Not yet," she said, in a tone that was half defiance, half request.

"Come on—"

"You'll have to save me first."

"What?"

"You save everyone else, Mr. Lifeguard," she teased. "Save me too."

"Out—or your folks will kill me."

She hesitated, treading the water perfectly. The uniform ripples pushed toward Max.

"Anabelle—"

"All right," and she paddled toward her clothes.

Anabelle, Max repeated as he pushed up from under the tree. As he watched her dress, he felt an uncontrollable shudder. It was hard taking his eyes away. He finally turned and powered himself up the slope, skirting behind a ridge so he wouldn't be spotted. He waited until their car streaked past him before he returned to the hotel grounds. Bright spotlights were everywhere. He hoped a night watchman wouldn't stop him and ask questions, maybe report him to management. But there was no one around.

His quarters were dark. Soft snoring rose up from the bunks. The cabin held six, and the last two boys had arrived late that afternoon. Max hadn't really talked to anyone yet. He groped his way to his bed, dropped on the cold mattress, and pulled up a sheet. Unable to sleep.

Anabelle, he thought.

It was the most beautiful name he had ever heard.

CHAPTER 2

Reggie Harrison's stomach was so full of butterflies he could hardly breathe. He moved in lockstep behind the other boys from his cabin as they were led through the cavernous kitchen. He had never seen a kitchen with not one but three freezer lockers, endless rows of stainless steel counters, more sinks, cooking grills and storage shelves than a whole town would need. As the five boys moved along, chefs in starchy white uniforms and towering hats were opening oven doors. A little after six, the sun was barely up, but from the kitchen activity it was difficult to tell. Reggie felt hopelessly tired and disoriented. His mother hadn't driven him down from Troy until late yesterday. Nervous about his first summer job, and meeting the new boys in his cabin, he'd slept poorly.

"I want your undivided attention, please. This is *extremely* important."

Mr. Carlton's cold voice was like a pinprick in the back. Reggie came to a halt with the others. He was afraid of screwing up and calling attention to himself. Nothing could be worse, he thought. He stared raptly at the thin, gaunt-faced man with the network of red vessels running under his cheeks, impeccably dressed in a gray suit and navy tie. The crease in his pants was so sharp you could cut your finger on it. Carlton's hands sliced the air decisively as he spelled out kitchen procedures. Where to find plates and utensils. What chef one brought meal orders to. Which counter to pick up the food. Where to bring dirty plates. If there was a mistake in taking an order, or a guest was displeased with the food, there were procedures, too. Carlton spoke authoritatively. He was someone you wanted to please, Reggie guessed, as he took in the rigid posture and observant eyes, or at least someone you didn't want to displease.

"Pick up a serving tray, young man. And tell me your name—"

It was a long agonizing moment when Reggie realized that Carlton was addressing him. Reggie gave his name but his voice sounded puny. Everyone stared as he bent down to the row of trays. It weighed a ton, he thought, as he perched one on his shoulder. Carlton showed him how to position his hand for better leverage, and then, without warning, began to pile dishes on top of Reggie's tray.

"A serving tray can comfortably hold eight dinner plates, if stacked properly, or eight soup bowls and salad plates together, or other assortments . . ."

Reggie's shoulder began to sag under the growing weight. He pushed one leg out for support, hoping that Carlton would stop, but the dishes kept coming. Was Carlton picking on him because of his slender build, maybe trying to scare him off before his job even began? His breathing came in coarse spurts and sweat beaded on his cheeks. Reggie felt everyone's eyes parading over him. He wanted to crawl in a hole and disappear.

When he glanced up, however, Carlton and the other boys were actually staring away. The food services manager helped ease the tray off Reggie's shoulder, his eyes still on the intruder. Reggie recognized the boy from his cabin. The one who'd sneaked out last night and returned very late, stumbling into Reggie's bunk before finding his own.

"And who are you?" Carlton asked, a razor edge to his voice.

"Max Riley, sir. I'm really sorry I'm late. I had some stomach problems this morning. You know how it is . . . wasn't feeling very hot, sir."

Reggie doubted he was really sick. Tired from last night, Max had probably just overslept. Though in his waiter uniform of dark slacks, white dress shirt and bow tie, like the others, Max looked sleepy and it was obvious he'd hurried to dress. Still, there was something special about him, Reggie thought, even if he couldn't pinpoint what it was. He had a broad Irish face with a faint band of freckles on his forehead, and a finely chiseled nose that gave him a refined air. He looked physically dangerous. A muscular torso, a tree trunk of a neck, calf muscles that bulged his slacks and looked almost the size of Reggie's thighs.

"We have a nurse on the premises," Carlton finally replied. He studied Max carefully, deciding not so much whether to believe him, Reggie guessed, as whether to give him another chance. "If you're sick, you sign in at the infirmary. *That is procedure* . . ."

"Yes, sir."

"Pull yourself together, Mr. Riley, and we'll continue the orientation. Unless, of course, you think we should all leave our shirttails out . . ."

The joke caught everyone by surprise, and as the laughter came in spurts it broke the tension. Maybe Carlton wasn't a total jerk, Reggie considered, relieved, though he still had plenty of doubts about the summer ahead. Working at the Sherborne was actually his mother's idea, or maybe she got it from the psychiatrist. After his father's death in a car accident last Christmas, Reggie had gone into a shell. Why *his* father? Why at Christmas? Why when they'd just had a big argument over nothing and his father had stormed out? A thousand whys, and no one, not even the psychiatrist chosen for Reggie, had convincing answers.

After the funeral, Reggie had begun staying home on weekends, dropping old friends, falling behind in schoolwork. Nothing really mattered. He didn't even want to care. He had the sense that no matter what he tried to do, it wouldn't work. And why should he worry about anybody else? The world was an unpredictable mess. He wanted a breather.

You're only hurting yourself, his mother warned as the months dragged on. You have to stop brooding. Keeping busy is everything. But it sounded to Reggie like she was giving advice to herself. Finally she made him go to sessions with a psychiatrist. The message was similar. Try something. Get involved with a hobby, a sport, people. Then, how about a summer job?

The Sherborne wasn't too far away. Reggie's mom was sure he'd make new friends with the other waiters. Only Reggie knew better. He would get along with everyone, not making waves, just like he did at school, but basically he wanted to be left alone.

Yesterday, after unpacking, he'd taken a stroll through Barnswell, liking it even less than the hotel or his cabin. Barnswell was one of those conservative upstate towns that every summer was invaded by wealthy outsiders. After the Sherborne, the reason people came was the lake. It nestled below the town in an almost perfect oval and was ideal for swimming and water-skiing. Unlike most mountain lakes, Chicopee was supposed to be warm, free of algae, and you could see your toes when you treaded water. The town proper wasn't exactly without charm either—or wealth. Large, brightly painted houses with white picket fences overwhelmed Reggie wherever he walked.

Downtown, in the shopping area, it could have been Manhattan's Upper East Side. Stylish boutiques, outdoor cafes, European pastries and ice cream. Everything was too expensive, for him anyway. And too many good-looking people to go with the good-looking shops. Lean, bronzed boys with tousled hair. Girls in bikinis, whose figures were coldly perfect. Reggie felt like a hopeless misfit. Better to stay in his cabin in his free time and read paperbacks than to get involved with anyone.

"Clean uniforms must be worn every day. The laundry opens from two to five every afternoon, which coincides with your time off. Everyone must be back to set tables for dinner *no later than five-fifteen—*"

The smell of bacon was everywhere. The rule, *the procedure*, Reggie remembered, was that waiters couldn't eat until after service hours, which for breakfast wasn't until ten. Reggie wondered if he would last. When the orientation was finally over, Carlton assigned the six boys to different tables. For the first day they were to assist the more experienced waiters, learning the ropes. Tomorrow they'd be on their own.

The pace in the kitchen was accelerating. Waiters streamed in to place orders and pick up their food. Reggie trailed behind a pale, overweight boy who said he'd been working at the Sherborne for four summers. He made Reggie carry his food trays. It was traditional for all newcomers, the boy explained, poker-faced, but Reggie didn't believe him. In the dining room his eyes kept cutting to the other boys from his cabin. Was he doing as well as they? The black kid named Washington looked as if he was in agony. Tall and moon-faced, he had seemed physically capable in the cabin, even athletic, but now his step was awkward, his tray balanced unsteadily on his bony shoulder.

"Are you okay?" asked Reggie, when they were back in the kitchen. The boy nodded. Reggie didn't feel overly sorry for anyone, but he sensed Washington wanted some sympathy.

"Oh, man, my back's on fire," he moaned.

"Sorry," Reggie said.

"Not as sorry as me. And I'm hungry. Aren't you hungry?"

Reggie watched as Washington hoisted up a full tray and lurched back into the dining room. His shoes squeaked. Like a gyroscope, the tray began to wobble, its slow-motion teetering building a momentum of its own. Washington let out a small, hoarse cry and his eyes dilated in panic. Diners swung their heads around. Washington's body had turned into Jell-O. One knee sagged, then the other.

From nowhere two large, sure hands seized the tray and retrieved it from danger. Max smiled at his audience as he rebalanced the tray in his own shoulder, and took a half bow. He was being a ham, Reggie thought, but it was a neat trick just the same.

Still clowning, Max never saw the approaching waiter. The collision was instantaneous with useless warning shouts from diners. The other waiter literally bounced off Max, whose body was like a bank-vault door, and collapsed on the floor. Plates soared up and clattered together, breaking, showering down like confetti. Diners shielded their heads or twisted away. One woman was cut on the cheek.

Surveying the damage, Max looked stunned and not a little sorry. Carlton's bony hand was suddenly on his shoulder, a grip so rigid that Reggie and everyone else knew. Max's summer at the Sherborne had just come to an end.

CHAPTER 3

Big trouble, Max thought. He followed Carlton through the marble and carved stone lobby and along a plushly carpeted corridor with mahogany doors that shined like brass. Carlton's office was spacious and regal. Expensive furniture, photos of Carlton shaking hands with famous guests. The view from the window framed the hotel beach and lake, but half-closed shutters were drawn across it.

Max took a seat and silently went over his options. He could tell the food manager to kiss off, returning to Bradley for the summer; only there was no way to earn decent money there. He could blame the collision on the other waiter, protest if Carlton fired him, and appeal to a higher-up. Or he could endure a tongue-lashing, as he often did with his football coach when Max missed practice, and wait for a reprieve. It usually came.

"I want you to know, Mr. Carlton," Max volunteered, "that I'm terribly sorry for what happened in there. Entirely my fault, sir. I was careless and not paying attention. I did help Washington, of course, but that's another matter . . ."

The somber figure sat across from Max with his fingers spread out in a web under his chin, as if lost in thought. He was like a stone, a monument, Max considered, to the decades of running the hotel's food services. No doubt he did it well, but he seemed to take everything so seriously.

From the gray, blotchy face it was doubtful Carlton ever stepped on the beach. It probably took a natural disaster to get him out of the hotel.

"It won't happen again. I can assure you," Max spoke into the void.

"No, I should think not."

More silence. What did Carlton mean? If he wanted to can Max, why didn't he come out and say it? "I was wondering, sir, what you're going to do."

Carlton's face began to relax. It still wasn't a warm face, but it was softer than in the kitchen, more flexible. Wheels were turning, Max suddenly realized.

"I don't think you're going to be happy at the Sherborne," Carlton began. "You were late to the kitchen this morning. Just now you dropped a tray and injured a guest. And last night you ignored curfew and romped around the lake—"

"Oh, no sir. Not me." Max did his best to sound confident. How did Carlton know? Maybe a night watchman saw him after all, or maybe his eminence here was bluffing. "I'm extremely happy at the Sherborne."

"Let's be honest, Mr. Riley. You're unhappy. You dislike the hotel and its staff. You find your lodging inferior. You think you deserve something better—"

Beautiful, thought Max. Carlton was playing psychologist. So many people in power did, like half the teachers in his school. This inquisition was for Carlton's sake, a way of toying with Max, putting him down. Punishment.

"Frankly, Mr. Carlton. I love it here." Max smiled for his interrogator. If this was a game, he could play, too. "I mean, to work at the Sherborne is a privilege."

"You like being a waiter here?"

"Of course. That's the job I applied for."

"Why a waiter?"

"I don't have to be a waiter, I suppose," he answered carefully. "I just believe it's necessary to work."

"Necessary for what?"

"The experience. One should get an idea of the real world, don't you think, sir? And for one's growth as an individual . . ." Why did he keep calling Carlton 'sir'? Just more of the bull Max was laying on. It was piling up so thick in here he could hardly breathe.

"What a refreshing attitude," Carlton observed. "Frankly, most boys come here for the money. The tips. They'll do most anything for a good tip. Indeed, they don't appreciate the traditions of this hotel. The generation of young people today only thinks of itself. 'What's in this for me? Why help someone else? To hell with the establishment.' "

His face actually showed a sneer. Carlton's emotion startled Max. "Terrible," he agreed.

"But you're different, Mr. Riley?"

"Yes, sir."

"Are you aware that we have *another* dining room at the Sherborne?" he said suddenly.

Max cleared his throat. What was this guy leading to? "No, sir."

"A private dining room. It's primarily for the residents of this town. You see, certain Barnswell families have been buying summer memberships at the Sherborne for years. They can use the beach, the hotel's facilities, enjoy its cuisine. They prefer dining apart from the hotel's regular guests. For one thing, they all know each other, and for another, it's more intimate in the smaller dining room. And they do pay a princely sum for their memberships . . ."

"I understand."

"Tradition," Carlton emphasized.

Max repeated the word.

"We have only a handful of waiters in our private dining room. It's not so busy. Conscientious employees with good attitudes . . ."

"That could be me," Max volunteered.

"It will be you. That's the job I want you to have."

Carlton suddenly gestured that the waiter could leave. As Max rose he smiled to himself. He was the winner here. He had his job back. He thought again of all the money he'd make.

The cold voice stopped him a final time by the door. "There's something you should know, Mr. Riley. Our Barnswell guests enjoy special privileges with their memberships."

"That's fine," Max said, not really caring.

"You should know what they are."

He notched his head up in curiosity. "All right."

"It's one privilege in particular I was thinking of."

"What's that, sir?"

"They don't have to tip."

CHAPTER 4

"eeeee . . . yyiiii . . . ouuuEEEE . . ."

Tiny Jenkins' mock howls bounced off the bathroom walls. As Max and the other boys washed up before the dinner shift, Tiny's blubbery figure dashed in and out of the shower. The fat rippled in his thighs and belly like miniature waves. "How can they expect a civilized human being to take cold showers?" he protested through the spray. "Barbarians!"

"They specialize in torture here," Max added, trying to shave. He was still upset after the reassignment from Carlton, though Max conceded he was at least partly at fault. He clowned around too much in his life and inevitably asked for trouble. Sometimes he came out ahead, sometimes he didn't. This time he'd had a set back. At least the events of the day had proved to be an icebreaker. For two hours the cabin had discussed nothing but the dining room collision and Max's new assignment. A lot of yucking it up as Tiny had imitated the food manager by sucking in his cheeks and puffing out his chest. Max couldn't quite see the humor, however. Without any tips now, he might as well pack it in and split for home. Some summer.

"You know, I really wanted to be a lifeguard," Tiny announced to everyone as he toweled off. "I filled out an application in December. Instead, they made me a waiter. I figured they thought my physique would gross out all the young, rich lovelies."

"What's the big deal about being a lifeguard?" Max interrupted. "You like wearing a whistle around your neck?"

"Love it. But I love the money even more."

"What would you make?" Max had never thought of applying for the position, though he was a good swimmer. "Same as waiters?"

"Ha!" said Tiny. "Try four times as much as being a waiter. Lifeguarding is considered skilled labor because you have to be certified by the Red Cross. Even counting in our tips, lifeguards are probably still ahead. And what do they do? No one's drowned in Lake Chicopee in forty years. Those guys just sit in their little white towers and bronze their bodies all day. Girls come up and rub against their legs. Tough life, gentlemen."

"Four times as much?" an astonished Max repeated. He slipped out of the bathroom and flopped on his bunk. "Why didn't you get the job?"

"I talked to some waiters who've been here a couple summers. Lifeguard jobs always go to rich boys from Barnswell. Favorite sons, as it were."

"Do something about it," Max suggested. "Tell Carlton you want to be a lifeguard. Tell him it's unfair that the hotel only hires locals—it's discriminatory."

"That's real cute. After what *you* went through today?"

Laughter. No one thought Max was serious. The other boys shuffled around, already used to the routine. Even Tiny, despite his humorous grousing, would fall into the rut. He wasn't the type to rebel, Max sensed. A nice enough kid, but hardly a mover and a shaker. After finishing school he'd probably wind up running the grocery store he said his family owned in Vermont.

"Hey, what about you, Washington?" Max asked. "Why are you working?"

"My father didn't want me around this summer. You know the jive—get a job, stay out of trouble . . ."

"Aw, come on Washington, tell the truth," Tiny deadpanned. "You like working here because of the whirlpool baths and midafternoon massages. Or is it the candlelight dinners?"

"You can keep the candles," Washington answered. "My stomach just wants a good meal. Guests eat steak but the help's fed meatloaf. Those little boiled potatoes we had for lunch? Those weren't nothin' but deep-fried golf balls . . ."

Laughter again. No one got the message, Max thought. They'd kid themselves through the summer, never quite waking up to the fact that being waiters was all they were good for. In their heart of hearts, that was all they wanted to be. There wasn't an ounce of ambition apparent in the cabin, Max decided as he glanced around. Kenny Homer was a decent looking kid from a town not far from Max's, tall and blond with good-fairy blue eyes, but he admitted he was a straight arrow, real salt of the earth. He went to church regularly, never argued with his parents or kicked his dog, and had been going steady with the same girl since junior high. Philip Lineberry was cut from a different cloth, a Massachusetts blue blood and the son of a fourth-generation preppie. To the family's disappointment, Philip was a hardcore goof-off, so his folks had sent him to work at the Sherborne to learn some discipline. Then there was that frail-looking kid with the nervous brown eyes, Reggie Harrison. On the surface he was pleasant enough, almost too agreeable, it seemed to Max. Sometimes he seemed in a daze, but maybe underneath he had potential. Max could only hope. Someone in the cabin had to be his ally.

Max had been tempted to explain his own plans for the future but held back. How could these guys understand if they didn't have any dreams of their own? When he got to California he was going to take the state real estate exam and become a sales broker. He was young, but Max knew he was good looking, and with his silver tongue he could sell anything. He'd read about the prices of houses in Southern California. It didn't take a genius to figure commissions on half-million dollar homes. All he had to do was get through this summer and another year at school. At one time he had actually considered going to college, but four years and then what? College would be a waste of time.

When it was time for the dinner shift, Max let the others walk ahead as he took a separate path to the smaller dining room. His fellow waiters were already there, putting fresh linen and silver on the tables. Older than the boys in the cabins, most were full-time Sherborne employees on annual salaries. Max felt like an oddity. He set his two tables, then, following procedure, stood quietly against a wall, hands behind his back.

His body suddenly stiffened as the first diners trickled in. He stared, disbelieving, at the party of four, focusing on the girl in particular. The girl in the lake. Anabelle. It had to be. Trailing behind her parents she was taller, more graceful, even prettier than last night. Her blond hair was like silk, dropping softly over her shoulders, and her face, with its well-proportioned features, could have belonged to a model. She was almost too pretty. Large hazel eyes, high cheek bones, an infectious smile, peaches-and-cream complexion.

She had every right to be stuck up, Max considered, but instead there was something fun and adventurous about her, even mischievous. He could tell from the way she waved to a girlfriend across the room, from her walk, and the smile. Her parents looked in their early fifties, fit and well preserved. The mother was particularly attractive, the source of Anabelle's beauty. And right behind Anabelle was a boy. Hunter, of course. Fashionably thin with a good physique, an intelligent, angular face, sweeping blue eyes that took in everything. With his button-down shirt and tweed jacket he looked like Mr. Right. The all-American boy who had everything going for him.

Max wanted to pinch himself as the maître d' marched the party to his table. His lucky night, he felt it. With his most polished smile Max wished everyone a good evening, then, as Hunter hesitated, he took the opportunity to seat Anabelle. She twisted back her head for the briefest of seconds, studying him. There was a click, he thought. A small, almost imperceptible click of approval.

Starting with Anabelle's mother, Max crisply unfolded the cloth-bound menus and cleared his throat. The house dressing was a blend of five spices and came in a vinaigrette. The cucumber vichyssoise had been a secret recipe in the chef's family for a century. There were a half-dozen special entrees for the evening, including poached trout. Handing the wine list to Anabelle's father, Max recommended a light, dry Chablis from California that was equal to anything from France. His tone was perfect, the right blend of knowledge and suggestion.

When the food was ready, Max served each course and stepped away decorously, joining the other waiters in a corner of the room. His head turned casually from Anabelle, but a wandering eye continually brought her into focus. The table conversation came in snippets, telegraphic bursts of information that Max eagerly absorbed. Anabelle was sixteen, had no brothers or sisters, and would return to her private all-girls boarding school in the fall. Father's surname was Livingston, owned a lot of upstate property and several businesses. Mother was into charity fund raisers. Max couldn't believe it. The Livingston family wasn't just from Barnswell, it was from *old* Barnswell, descendents of a signer of the Declaration of Independence. All the time Hunter said little, a polite "yes" or "no," or a "I don't believe so, sir," and a couple of bland anecdotes about being a lifeguard. Max noticed that Hunter's hand, busier than his mouth, had carefully sneaked under the table to find Anabelle's.

Halfway through the evening, Max came to attention again. Carlton strolled into the dining room along with another gentleman named Fitzroy, the top lieutenant under the hotel's owner, Max remembered from orientation. After a prolonged study of the room, they settled at Max's second table. He wasn't surprised. Hotel management ate in the same room as Barnswell members, and what better chance for Carlton to check on his prodigal waiter than to choose his table? Max's only regret was he couldn't devote full time to Anabelle. He glided between the two parties, letting the food manager's eyes parade over him without fear. His clothes were neat, shoes polished, tie straight. And he knew the menu as well as anyone. Nothing was going to happen to him, not on his lucky night. Fitzroy, jowly and red-cheeked, complimented him twice, and even Carlton managed an affable smile.

"Sir, may I read you the dessert menu for this evening?" Max said to Anabelle's father when it was time. He stood to the right of Mr. Livingston, so his eye could lift unobtrusively to Anabelle. She was really gorgeous. No girl around Bradley or anywhere else Max had been came even close to her. "We have a delightful chocolate mousse, lightly laced with rum . . . fresh peach tart . . . a whipped meringue on a half pastry shell . . . fudge layer cake . . ." The words suddenly locked in his throat. Anabelle had caught him looking. Instead of turning her eyes away, she kept staring at him. It was almost a dare, a game, to see who would turn his head away first.

"How many calories in that cake, would you say?" Anabelle's mother asked playfully to Max and everyone at the table.

Max took a breath and let his eyes swim to her in a reprieve. "A small slice, ma'am, wouldn't do anyone great harm."

"How diplomatically put," she said. "I'll take the smallest slice you have."

Max memorized the orders and brought in the desserts with coffee. He was afraid to look at Anabelle again. When everyone had finished he cleared the table and gave Mr. Livingston the check to sign.

"Let me help you," Max said, pulling back Anabelle's chair to let her out.

"Thank you." Her voice was pure gold. "What's your name?"

His heart jumped, even more than at the lake. "Max. Max Riley."

"Are you here for the summer?"

"That's right. The whole summer."

Hunter started to nudge her away, but Anabelle resisted. "First time in Barnswell?"

He nodded. "But not my last."

Anabelle cocked her head, as if the answer amused her. "Well, it's nice meeting you."

Max was smiling, entranced, when he felt a hand on his elbow. Oh no, he thought, afraid to turn. But when he did, it was only Anabelle's father. A hand was extended, as though to shake Max's, only the palm was closed.

"Terrific service," he said. At the next table Carlton was looking over. Max thought the food manager would have a cardiac arrest. "Really first rate," Mr. Livingston added, peering over his glasses. And with a pat on the shoulder, he pushed a twenty into Max's hand.

CHAPTER 5

Max stood impatiently near the short picket fence that separated the city beach from the hotel's. As the sun hammered down, his eyes continued to parade over the Sherborne beach. In fifteen minutes he had to shower and change for the evening shift—so where was Anabelle? Since serving her dinner two nights ago, he'd spent most of his free time trying to find her, annoyed with the rule that forbid him to cross over onto the hotel beach. He felt a little resentful, and self-conscious as an outsider. Ready to give up, his eye suddenly caught a group of girls in jeans and bikini tops as they walked down from the shore road, their noses whitened with sun screen but otherwise sporting perfect tans. He peered more closely, focusing on one blond who held a kitten in her arms. Then Max spotted the key around her neck. Anabelle, at last, he thought, and his spirits lifted.

"Hi!" Max shouted, raising a muscular arm in the air. He caught Anabelle's attention just as she handed over the kitten to a friend and was ready to slip into the water. She glanced up, struggling to recognize Max, and finally strolled toward the picket fence.

"Hello," she answered, without coming too close. She pushed a hand through her long silky hair as she studied Max. He was confident he'd check out just fine. No one on either beach had a better physique.

"Remember me?" Max said cheerfully when the silence lingered.

She looked puzzled, then shook her head.

"From the hotel restaurant—"

"Oh." Anabelle pushed a finger to her lips. "Max, isn't it?" she said.

"Terrific. What a memory," he joked, trying to break the tension. Anabelle didn't return the smile. Maybe he was coming on too strong. That was the only style he knew. "I've been looking for you, you know," he added.

"Really?"

"I thought I could get to know you."

"Me?" she said.

She looked surprised. Was she about to laugh? "That is, if you don't mind—"

"Mind what?"

"That I get to know you. That we're talking now. That the next time we meet I might be really impulsive . . ." Max beamed.

Anabelle folded her arms, looking Max in the eye, like she had at the restaurant. "Are you making a pass at me?" The tone was of polite disbelief, and slightly cold.

Max only shrugged. Anabelle was being difficult, a contrast to what he'd thought was her openness at the restaurant. Maybe, in truth, she didn't like outsiders. Maybe she was a Barnswell snob after all. "Sure," he finally said. "I'm making a pass. What else am I supposed to do—ignore you?"

She studied him coolly for a moment, as if making up her mind. Suddenly she tossed back her head and a smile appeared. "Well, at least you're honest."

"As the day is long," he chimed in. And down deep, he thought, he really was. Maybe he threw the bull pretty well, but that didn't mean he couldn't be sincere when it counted. "Do you like honesty in people?" he added.

"As a matter of fact, I do. And a sense of humor. I like to have fun."

"My friends say I'm the wittiest guy they know," Max volunteered, though at the moment he couldn't think of a single funny line. "I was wondering," he offered, rocking back on his heels, "if you'd like to see a movie tonight."

"You're asking me out? I hardly know you."

"That's why I'm asking—so you can."

"You're fast."

"Like I said the other night, I'm only here for the summer."

"Tonight?"

"After I get off work. About nine?"

"Thanks," she said sweetly, "but I promised my friends I'd go with them." Max followed her gaze back to the hotel beach. Her girlfriends were staring at them, whispering among themselves.

"Maybe some other time," Max said.

"Maybe."

"How about the weekend?"

"We'll see."

"You mean, if your boyfriend doesn't mind." Max focused on Hunter's tower. It was vacant at the moment.

Anabelle's face tightened in surprise. "Why should I check with Hunter? He doesn't own me. I do what I like."

"Of course you do," Max said agreeably.

"Well, so long." But after a few steps Anabelle turned around again, smiling mischievously. "You know," she called out, "you're different. I like that."

Max waved. Then, with great reluctance, he marched back up the beach toward his cabin. He wondered if his little chat with Anabelle could be rated a success. She had come across as a little coy and evasive, but that was probably just a game. Max knew he'd done all right. The test came when she'd turned him down for the movie and, without blinking, he'd asked for another date. Girls liked that kind of self-confidence. And Max liked Anabelle's independence. No, he felt fine. He smiled to himself. Anabelle could be won over in a big way this summer. He was sure of it.

Whistling cheerfully, he pushed open the cabin door. He focused on the trip wire just as the door hit it. Except to cover his head, he had no other time to react. The serving trays clattered down like miniature flying saucers, an avalanche that clanged all around him. One bounced harmlessly off his shoulder and rolled right back out the door. Tiny's head peeked up first, then several of the other boys, their faces breaking into laughter.

"Hey, we thought you were Carlton," someone said. "He was supposed to inspect the cabins."

Max smiled indifferently and flopped down on his bunk. The door could have been rigged to a land mine and he doubted that he would have noticed. The only thing that mattered right now was Anabelle—pretty, pretty, Anabelle. Light of his life. Fount of his dreams.

CHAPTER 6

The kitten was driving Hunter bananas. Whimpering, scratching his bare legs, nearly jumping off the tower. Anabelle had dumped the spoiled pet in his lap and promised to be back by four, but now it was pushing six and the lake had mostly emptied. The last of the swimmers and water-skiers shuffled by the lifeguard tower to glance curiously at the gold and brown kitten. Embarrassed, Hunter didn't feel like explaining. He just wanted Anabelle to retrieve her dumb cat and never bring it to the beach again.

Seizing the animal in one hand, Hunter Braxton clambered down the tower and scanned the lake for delinquent swimmers. The hotel closed its beach every evening at six, which was fine with Hunter and his friends, because nights were the best part of summers in Barnswell. Lifeguarding wasn't exactly painful—besides a good tan, Hunter liked the idea that people looked up to him—but the day often seemed endless. Lifeguards were on duty six days a week, nine to six, getting only Tuesdays off, when the hotel allowed the beach to stay open but disclaimed any responsibility for guests and members. What made the season even longer was the daily boredom. In three summers at Lake Chicopee Hunter hadn't saved more than a dozen swimmers, efforts that were hardly dramatic—paddling out thirty yards and tossing preservers to kids with cramps. Real ho-hum. Still, when Hunter got back to Andover every fall, he milked the episodes for all they were worth.

A small, brownish head bobbed up and down at the south end of the beach, near the string of buoys that separated the swimming area from the boat docks. Impatient, Hunter hurried over to wave the kid out, glancing back at the lake road to check again for Anabelle. Traffic was typically heavy for the summertime. The rows of houses behind the shore road shimmered in the heat haze, blurring as one. For a moment, as Hunter stared carefully, he picked out Anabelle's house with its white windows and sea-green shutters and pitched roof. It was a stunning house, one of the largest in Barnswell, and he visited there, with the approval of Anabelle's parents, as often as he could.

But it wasn't often enough, not for Hunter. The home, twice the size of his own, which wasn't exactly shabby, was magnificent, filled with Revolutionary and Civil War antiques. Not only was Hunter fond of its beauty and comforts, he liked hanging around Anabelle's parents. Hunter went out of his way to be polite and helpful, acting like the young gentleman, because it was what impressed them most. Mr. Livingston, while usually affable, judged everyone by fairly strict standards, especially his daughter's boyfriend. Hunter was careful not to disappoint him. That's why they got along. It also didn't hurt Hunter's relationship with Anabelle for her parents to speak well of him.

"Hey—come on! Beach's closed!" Hunter shouted, waving his arms through the air for emphasis. When the little girl didn't respond, Hunter felt annoyed—sheer disbelief that he wasn't noticed. Finally he slipped his silver whistle between his lips and blew sharply. The girl twisted her head up, smiled an apology, and scampered toward her beach towel. Hunter liked that, the authority his whistle conveyed, that he himself embodied. Over the summers he'd come to think of Lake Chicopee almost as his own, a private territory that, as head lifeguard, he dominated as he pleased. True, it was the hotel that hired him and made the rules about swimming hours and excessive noise and no drinking by the lake, but without Hunter or his friends to enforce them, the Sherborne could stuff the rules in a dusty drawer somewhere.

With a final twist of his head Hunter was satisfied that the lake was clear, and that the hotel's motorboats had been properly moored in their berths. He flexed his toes in the sand. For appearance sake, the hotel some years ago had brought in white sand to make the lake beach more like an ocean's. Hunter liked that. There was just something pure and clean about the look. The kitten still under his arm, he glanced up as two tall, broad-shouldered boys in jeans and designer shirts kicked a soccer ball back and forth, moving briskly along the beach. Hunter marveled at how quickly Toby and Skip, and the two other lifeguards as well, could change clothes. All day they sat up in their towers, too lazy to budge, but at six it was like someone had lit a fire under their butts.

"Hustle up," Skip hollered, as he sliced the ball neatly off his foot to Hunter. A six-pack was under his arm. "Maybe we'll have time to horse around a little before hitting Lord Michael's."

"I'm waiting for Anabelle," Hunter answered, half trying to hide the stupid cat behind his back. Resigned, he finally dropped it at his feet.

"I thought I saw a puddy tat," Toby mimicked.

Skip joined the laughter. "Hey, Hunter, holding out on us?"

Hunter wished he could get rid of the cat and join them. Something told him Anabelle wouldn't show. She was often late, and sometimes so dizzy she forgot dates and appointments altogether. It drove him up the wall. Skip and Toby were constant and more reliable. The three boys had grown up together and now attended the same prep school. Unlike Hunter, who took grades seriously, Skip and Toby were more carefree. They were basically bright and probably would get into good colleges, but they lacked Hunter's intensity.

"Come on, Hunter. Forget Anabelle for once," Toby prodded.

He hesitated, but finally shook his head. "Listen, I'll meet you at the pub in an hour."

Hunter watched them leave, feeling frustrated again. Was Anabelle going to stand him up? Maybe she didn't really care if she kept him waiting. Lately she had been acting independent, too independent to Hunter's thinking. She didn't visit him on the beach as often as last summer, preferring her girlfriends as company. And her new game was carrying a little kitten all over town. All of which meant she wasn't paying enough attention to Hunter. A couple of nights ago, in the hotel restaurant, she had practically put her arms around that hulk of a waiter. Didn't she realize that Hunter would mind? The next day he put the damper on any more meals at the Sherborne. She couldn't understand why. "I don't like you flirting with other guys," he finally admitted, trying not to sound too jealous.

Anabelle had acted amused, and unconcerned. But Hunter knew he had to put his foot down to show her who was boss. He couldn't risk losing Anabelle. They had met at the exclusive Barnswell Fourth of July dance three years ago. He had decided it was love and thought she had too. He needed her. She represented so much he wanted to be sure he was a part of. One day, after college, he'd probably marry her.

Toby and Skip had reached the shore road when Toby spun around, cupping his hands around his mouth. "Hey, Hunter—forgot to tell you! Starting next week, we have to work Tuesdays, too! Full seven-day weeks. Just like the waiters. Us poor, miserable, downtrodden lifeguards . . ."

"What?" Hunter shouted back, not believing what he was hearing.

"I was told at lunch," Toby called. "Something about a lawsuit against the hotel . . . because the beach wasn't supervised all the time. So now we have to be around every day until six—"

Hunter said nothing, waving his friends on, but he was angry. It was incredible. The hotel wanted them to work seven days a week? Why hadn't he been consulted? How was it that Toby heard before him? He was the head lifeguard, wasn't he? The hotel couldn't do this unilaterally. Of course, Skip and Toby could care less. They sat around the lake on Tuesdays anyway, and sometimes so did Hunter and Anabelle. But what they didn't comprehend was that there was a principle here, a matter of honor. Someone just didn't start rearranging your life—not without asking if it was okay first.

Tomorrow he'd make it a point to see Fitzroy. Nobody was going to have to work Tuesdays. Hunter Braxton would see to it.

As Hunter turned, he accidentally stepped on the kitten's tail. The piercing whine triggered a burst of fury in him. It was all he could do not to kick the little monster. As the unfocused anger settled, he realized who he was really annoyed with—Anabelle. What was her problem? And he was furious with the hotel for not consulting him; and Skip and

Toby were jerks too, for their indifference. He seized the kitten gruffly by its neck and walked to his tower. He climbed up for a better view. No Anabelle.

Something warm suddenly trickled down his thigh. He was horrified, as the cat's tail shivered straight up and its little back legs wobbled uncontrollably. For the love of— Enraged, Hunter grabbed the animal and hurled it through the air. He watched, both amused and mystified, as it landed twenty feet out in the lake, splashing down like a piece of wood. He hadn't meant to throw it that far.

The kitten's head bobbed up like a tiny buoy, twisting from side to side. Hunter wondered if cats could swim. Puppies could, almost from birth, he thought, but he wasn't sure about kittens. A voice told him to jump down and make his rescue, but something held him back. Let the little sucker fend for itself. It got what it deserved.

The cat began to struggle, pushing a paw hopefully above the water, like it was a surface to climb over or on top of. The blue floor suddenly gave way and the head dipped down. Then the water was still.

"Hunter!"

Startled, he turned to find Anabelle moving toward him in the distance. A convertible stood behind her, filled with her girlfriends, and they waved casually to Hunter before driving off. Anabelle hadn't seen him throw the cat, he realized, relieved. Her arms were crossed contemplatively over her chest and her head angled down to resist a lake breeze. The lacey blouse shifted back and forth. As usual, her house key dangled like a pendant from her neck—another little summertime quirk. Hunter waved from the lifeguard tower.

For a second her image transfixed him. He made out the aristocratic nose and the perfect white teeth that years of orthodontics had guaranteed. He studied her walk, the way she tossed back her head every few steps to let her hair bounce up and hang delicately in the air—frozen for an instant—and how her hips moved so sensually. She was his, he thought again. She made his life complete. He forgave her for being late.

"I'm sorry, I'm sorry," she breathed, half running as she neared him now. He leaped from the tower. "Mother asked me to run some errands and it took *ages*. Then the car died on me . . ."

She made a hopeless face. Anabelle could never figure out a car, or stop a leaky faucet or, Hunter doubted, even pound in a nail. Most girls today could do some of those things, proudly, but Anabelle was aloof from life's details. Her head was just somewhere else, or maybe she always expected someone to be around when she needed help.

Hunter smiled in sympathy. "It's okay. I'll look at the car."

They strolled down the beach. The wind had died to leave the lake's surface glass smooth and, in one corner, where the sun was hitting, diamond-fire bright. Hunter kissed her behind the ear.

"Where's Muffin?" she asked suddenly, turning to face him. He saw alarm and fear in her eyes. How crazy. It was just a kitten.

"Cat's fine," he lied. "I gave it to a little girl on the beach to hold."

"What girl?" she demanded, still upset.

"I don't know. She was the last one out of the lake."

"We have to find her."

"Don't worry."

"Let's look—"

"Hey, it's just a cat," he said as he slipped an arm around Anabelle. "We'll find Muffin tomorrow. Promise." Anabelle turned quiet. Hunter figured she was moping about the cat, and he ignored it. Maybe what he had done was rash and thoughtless, but that was history now. She'd get over it. Hunter let his thoughts drift to Anabelle. Her body felt incredible next to his, warm and full of mystery. He led her back to town, one hand playing with her hair, while Anabelle gazed at the ground, still quiet.

"Hey, penny for your thoughts," he said, smiling. When she didn't answer, he asked what was wrong.

"Nothing," she said, in a tone that perplexed him, "nothing at all. But don't forget about my kitten."

CHAPTER 7

The whine of mosquitoes filled the night air. Reggie lurched up from his bunk and made a desperate lunge, and in the process nearly tumbled off. Across the room, with his Walkman earphones looped around his head, Philip Lineberry smiled at the little drama.

"Hey, Reggie, got any Mars bars left?" Philip asked. The long, chiseled face and sad eyes had begun to remind Reggie of a horse.

"Let me look," he said, putting down the paperback novel. The two were alone in the cabin, but it still felt crowded to Reggie.

"Thanks."

"No problem."

Reggie dug into the care package his mom had sent down, tossed the candy bar to Philip, and went back to slapping mosquitoes. Only two weeks had passed and already his back looked like a pizza. The insect repellant sold in the hotel sundries shop smelled like barbecue sauce and worked just as well. Mosquitoes flocked to it. The itching was so bad he sometimes couldn't sleep. After dinner tonight, when the rest of the cabin had run off to Barnswell, Reggie had given Max a few bucks to buy some calamine lotion.

"Reggie, I hate to keep asking, but you wouldn't have any more taffy, would you? Just a couple pieces . . ."

"Sure. Hold on." Reggie flipped up the bite-size nougats

and watched as Philip tossed them into his mouth like popcorn. Philip was forever mooching—food, razor blades, toothpaste, shoelaces. Tiny had finally gotten pissed off one night after Philip had asked for his soap. What a parasite, he'd told everyone in front of Philip. This guy's family could afford the Brooklyn Bridge, and he's always looking for a handout.

Philip had said nothing, indifferently scooting to a corner of his bunk with a copy of *Playboy*, and putting on the Walkman earphones. Philip was lazy and a little arrogant, but his quirks bothered Reggie no more than Max slinging the bull, or Washington complaining, or Tiny telling fat boy jokes because he was fat himself. Nobody was perfect. After his father's death, Reggie kept his opinions to himself. He could get along with anybody so long as it meant no one bothered him. At school, teachers considered him unusually polite. Kids thought he was a nice guy. His mom and her friends found him thoughtful.

It was all part of the greatest act on earth, Reggie knew. After he'd decided to retreat from the world, what better way than to pretend to get along with everyone? Tell people what they want to hear and they'll leave you alone. Never reveal your true feelings. Never rock the boat. He could feign sympathy for Attila the Hun if he had to. Somebody should have nominated him for an Academy Award.

But while Reggie could fool people, he could never quite feel comfortable around them. So much pretending had put him at a distance. Sometimes his isolation bothered him. Sometimes he wanted a new friend. Despite his early feelings of caution, Reggie had considered Max a candidate. There was something bigger-than-life about Max, something bold; he didn't act afraid of anything. Reggie admired that because being fearless was something he wasn't. So far Reggie had failed to make any overtures, hanging back in his usual style. He wondered what Max thought about him.

Reggie checked the time again. Almost curfew. A hotel watchman had been making rounds of the cabins the last few nights. Things had been too calm and uneventful, which had probably made Carlton suspicious. But everything really *was* going smoothly. Bitching in the cabin had quieted down, and Max, of all people, was earning a reputation as the most conscientious waiter at the Sherborne, laying on his charm as thick as the icing on the fudge layer cake. In spite of the tradition of frugality of local members, he knew how to get tips. So far he'd hauled in over $300.

Even more important than the money, Max reported to everyone, he's fallen in love with a princess. The cabin had snickered in unison when he told his dinner story about Anabelle, and later finding her on the beach, but Max wasn't daunted. He wanted her, he said, and he always got what he wanted. He'd twice spotted Anabelle with her boyfriend, Hunter, and once in town while she shopped with her mother. Tiny warned that Max was out of his gourd to think he could get even close to her. A lousy waiter making it with the local goddess? Dream on. Reggie knew that Max didn't hear. He was the kind of boy who set goals for himself, and Anabelle had just been put at the top of the list.

With Max's spirits up, so were the cabin's. Everybody treated their jobs as a game, playing by Carlton's rules, but during breaks and after work they made up their own rules. It was Max's idea to organize waiters' volleyball and water polo on the public beach, where he deliberately razzed hotel lifeguards by kicking balls into their territory. Max loved it every time Hunter angrily blew his whistle at them. "What's he think this is," Max told everyone, "a private beach just for lifeguards?" Tiny and Washington, on their time off, usually went to a video arcade. There were always townies around looking to be challenged. Reggie had tagged along once, watching the bets pile up. When Tiny and Washington finally scored the most points, they took their winnings and splurged on steak dinners at an expensive town restaurant. Everyone suspected that Carlton knew about the little escapades, but there were no rules expressly forbidding them.

Putting down his book, Reggie moved outside. Philip had fallen asleep with his earphones on. There was still no sign of Max or the others and it was now after curfew. Maybe Max was testing the limits. Fine, but what if everyone got caught? Reggie and Philip might get in trouble too. Carlton would probably just as soon punish the entire cabin. While Reggie envied Max's boldness, it also bothered him sometimes. It was okay for Max to take the world by storm, but he didn't have the right to hurt everyone in the fallout.

The moon suddenly revealed a broad figure in the distance. Max was whistling cheerfully, blind to any danger, and carrying a lumpy package under one arm. His band of merry followers staggered behind. Only Kenny Homer looked halfway sober, Reggie saw as the group entered the cabin. He was surprised Kenny had drunk at all. Because he was such a straight arrow, Reggie had pegged him as a teetotaler. Max must have been pretty persuasive.

"Harrison, my man," said Washington, slapping Reggie's hands. "You missed out tonight . . ."

"Yeah, party pooper," Tiny seconded good-naturedly. He slumped on his bed. "There's this place called Lord Michael's. It's an English pub, with little golden-haired wenches serving pizza and beer. We told 'em we were all eighteen, and they believed us. We drank our brains out!"

"Sorry I wasn't there," said Reggie.

"Come on, you aren't sorry." Max stood at the doorway

to the john, opening his package. The calamine lotion came out first, and Reggie thanked him quietly. "You've never come to town at night," Max spelled out. His tone was more inquisitive than reproachful. "Not once."

"I wanted to finish my book," Reggie answered smoothly. For proof he held up the paperback.

"Maybe you just don't like having fun," Max challenged him.

"Sure I do. I play water polo with you—"

"But even then you look like you're in a trance. A thousand miles away. You go around acting as if everything is hunky-dory, but you're not with us, Harrison. Am I right or what?"

Caught off guard, Reggie turned away. Smiling anyway, Max popped open two cans of beer and offered one to Reggie.

"Come on," said Max, sitting on Reggie's bunk beside him. "You gotta relax. You gotta have fun in life."

"Sure," said Reggie, but his hand shook as he took the can. Washington flicked off the cabin lights and groped to his bed. The others had already sacked out.

"Here's to the future," Max toasted in the darkness.

"Right," Reggie echoed, but his voice betrayed him. He resented Max for being so forceful, picking on him. He pushed the can to his lips but didn't drink.

"What's the matter?" asked Max.

Reggie cleared his throat. "We're breaking a rule. No liquor on hotel premises . . ."

"Tsk-tsk. Breaking a rule. So what? Who cares?"

"You don't want to lose your job, do you?" Reggie said boldly.

"No one's going to lose his job. Carlton won't find out about the beer. You worry too much, Harrison."

"Maybe," he conceded. But he thought Max's tone was so

superior, and reckless. "I don't think what you did tonight was too thoughtful," he suddenly said, turning to Max. "You could have gotten caught and jeopardized the whole cabin. It was asking for trouble."

Max's smile was somewhere between astonishment and impatience. "Sure, sometimes I look for fun and that asks for trouble, but Harrison, you're the opposite. You go out of your way to avoid it. Like you're running from something. You're always uptight—"

The two boys suddenly froze. Outside, the sweep of a flashlight cut across the pines and spruces, and slowly swam to the cabin window. It hesitated, as if it had a will of its own, before floating on. Max sighed and leaned back. Soft snoring had begun to fill the silence. Slowly, Reggie drank his beer. He wasn't sure why. Maybe Max's taunting had finally gotten to him, or perhaps he wanted to show him he could drink a beer or two. But something else, too. He had spoken up, to Max's face no less. His own voice and its boldness had taken Reggie by surprise, but now he was relieved, almost proud of himself. And having said his piece, Reggie could see that Max had a point, too. He really was too uptight.

Max suddenly tapped his beer can against Reggie's, as if to make a toast. "You know, Harrison, this could be a great summer for you," he said in a hoarse whisper. "A breakthrough summer."

"What?"

"We're going to make you a new man."

Reggie said nothing, wondering.

"A new man," Max repeated, "with a new woman."

"What are you talking about?"

"I saw Anabelle tonight. She was with her girlfriends at the pub. When I finally got her alone, we hit it off beautifully."

"You were with Anabelle?" Reggie said, pleased for him.

"That's why I was late getting back."

"That's great, I guess," he added, trying not to sound too enthusiastic.

"I suggested we have a little party. Next Saturday night. Anabelle and her friends, and all of us in the cabin. A beach party. Small, intimate, away from the hotel, of course. Harrison, I spotted the girl for you right away."

Reggie nodded, afraid of what was coming. But Max's head suddenly lolled back against the pillow, and his eyes narrowed in drunkenness. The beer can began to slip from his hand. Reggie carefully stashed it under the bunk. In another minute Max was snoring. What had he meant—a girl for Reggie? Reggie wasn't sure he was ready. It was one thing to loosen up and have fun, another to bring a girl into the picture. And what about Anabelle's boyfriend? Max didn't seem to worry about the opposition. Maybe he was so nuts over Anabelle he didn't care, or maybe he was testing the limits again.

A concert of crickets filled the air. Reggie tried to move Max to his own bunk, but it was hopeless. It would have been easier lifting bags of cement. The best Reggie could do was raise Max's legs onto the mattress, wedge a pillow under his head, and slip off his shoes. Then he covered him with a blanket.

With his own shirt and pants off, Reggie dabbed on the calamine lotion, relishing the cool sensation. Max had been a lifesaver. The watchman's flashlight beam swept over the window again as Reggie flopped on Max's bunk, but now it seemed harmless. He closed his eyes.

This time he didn't have to count sheep.

CHAPTER 8

Hunter was losing his patience. For days Fitzroy's secretary had been telling Hunter that the hotel manager had no time to see the lifeguards.

"We'd still like to see Mr. Fitzroy," Hunter said coolly, as he waited in the manager's outer office. Skip and Toby hovered behind him. The hotel's mezzanine was staid and quiet, mostly executive and accounting offices, but Hunter was prepared to make a scene if he couldn't get in to Fitzroy. Last Tuesday, in spite of the new work policy, Hunter had convinced the other lifeguards to boycott the beach. Fitzroy then issued a written ultimatum: unless the lifeguards were prepared to put in seven-day weeks for the rest of the season, they would be dismissed. Incensed, Hunter had asked for a meeting with the hotel manager.

Nobody was going to be fired, Hunter felt confident. More importantly, he had decided not to give in to Fitzroy. It was a matter of principle. The hotel was trying to exploit the lifeguards, pure and simple, because it didn't care about the feelings or opinions of its employees. Hunter wanted more respect than that. He'd given three of his summers to the job, he'd saved lives, and not once had he gotten even a thank you. That wasn't Fitzroy's way. He took loyalty for granted.

"We're still waiting," said Hunter.

The secretary, a dimpled young woman with mouse-brown

hair, looked unhappy. "I'll ask Mr. Fitzroy again," she conceded, and retreated to the inner office.

It was early morning, but Hunter was sweating heavily. The ceiling fan whirred with a click-click-click. He glanced out to the elegant marble hallway, cracked from age like blocks of ice, and frowned at Toby and Skip. They looked bored as they shared a soft drink and made jokes. Why couldn't they understand the seriousness of the situation?

"All right, Mr. Fitzroy will see you now," the secretary said in a begrudging voice. Like some private guard, she held open the glass door. Hunter, emboldened, waved for Skip and Toby to follow.

What a relic, Hunter thought as his eyes met the manager's. The geezer had been Barnswell's mayor almost thirty years ago, and had gotten to be cozy with the hotel's owner. After he lost the election, he didn't worry about a new job. He took to the hotel and the hotel took to him. One of these days they'd have to bury him here. His favorite activity was to stuff himself with pasta dishes and rich pastries with enough calories to light up Manhattan. He had a wattle on his neck as thick as a turkey's.

"I think I should come straight to the point, Mr. Fitzroy," Hunter began. A radio was turned on low, some symphony that Hunter didn't recognize. "We represent the five lifeguards. We're upset over your decision to increase our work week."

Fitzroy took forever to clear his throat. "I understand your not being happy," he allowed, "but the hotel doesn't have much choice. We don't have the budget to hire extra lifeguards, so we're asking everyone to pitch in."

Fitzroy sounded sincere, but Hunter wasn't buying. Didn't have the budget, huh? What bull! This place was like Fort

Knox; the hotel could afford whatever it pleased. The truth was that management was just cheap. "I'd like to know why we weren't consulted about your decision," said Hunter.

"I do apologize, but you boys do work for us."

"And you expect us to work more hours without a pay increase?"

"Perhaps your salaries could be raised slightly. You have your evenings free. But I'll try to add an extra fifty dollars for the season."

"Fifty bucks?" Hunter said, outraged. "That's all? You've got to be kidding—"

"Some people say you're paid enough as it is, young man." Fitzroy's tone turned firmer.

"Sir, the name isn't young man. It's Hunter Braxton," he answered pointedly. Did this little manager not even know who he was? Incredible, after seeing Hunter around the hotel for three summers. "I'm afraid we can't accept the hotel's new policy. I speak for all the lifeguards. We're not working on Tuesdays. No way. And if you and the hotel keep insisting that we do, *we're going on strike*."

Fitzroy didn't seem to comprehend, or maybe he just didn't hear Hunter. Skip and Toby looked surprised. Hunter had saved his little bombshell as a final ploy, not divulging it to anyone. He had thought long and hard before making the threat. If a strike was called, Hunter knew there weren't many boys in Barnswell who would take the lifeguards' places. Most of the local kids were already busy for the summer and the few who might want the jobs Hunter would put pressure on to back off.

As if finally understanding, Fitzroy reared up from behind his desk and wagged a finger at Hunter. "You're no one special, young man. You can be replaced in an instant, just like this . . ." Two fingers snapped cleanly. "Now, you do yourself a favor and be on that beach Tuesday. Or else. *Au revoir, messieurs.*"

"*Au revoir,*" Toby whispered back, chuckling.

This guy was a half fruitcake, thought Hunter. Was that supposed to be French? Hunter bent over the desk to make sure Fitzroy heard him. "No guy or girl in town is going to replace us. You need us. We're indispensable." Fitzroy wouldn't look at him. "We're the only ones in town who'll work as lifeguards. I promise you. And without lifeguards the lake isn't safe. Even your attorneys said so. If an accident happens, the hotel gets sued. You need us—"

Fitzroy reached toward the radio and twisted up the volume until the music pounded in everyone's ears. The fossil sat back, smiling defiantly. Enraged, Hunter led his friends out of the hotel.

"What a bozo," he breathed, still fuming, as they moved in a phalanx toward the beach. "The hotel's not going to do this to us. I guarantee it."

"What are we going to do if they do?" Toby asked, as if he didn't like Hunter's threatening tone. "Listen, let's forget the strike. It's not worth it."

"And work Tuesdays?" Hunter said, incredulous.

"One extra day isn't going to kill us. The waiters do it."

"Yeah," Skip echoed. "Besides, Fitzroy isn't going to back down. The man is very serious. And I like my job."

"First of all, we're not waiters. We're lifeguards. That means we're better. Secondly, when will you guys get the point? The hotel is exploiting us. There's no respect—"

Hunter gave up. They'd never understand. Toby and Skip probably thought he was blowing things out of proportion, like they said he often did at school. He had a campus reputation for being high strung, someone who made issues out of things that didn't bother anyone else. He couldn't help it. He had high standards. If someone borrowed a book or clothes or money from Hunter, he had to return the item when promised or Hunter would never loan to him again. Half the kids were parasites. The problem was they had no pride in themselves, no self-respect. Look at the way they lived in the dorms, like pigs. Hunter thought of himself as better than the rest.

The beach was filling quickly. Hunter weaved between the stretched-out bodies to reach his tower. Motorboats were already streaking out to the middle of the lake, a good mile and a half from the shore, and closer in little kids were splashing around. Up in his tower Hunter tried to concentrate on the important things. The scenario was fairly predictable, he decided. As Skip had pointed out, Fitzroy wouldn't back down. But the lifeguards wouldn't capitulate either. Hunter would call for a strike, probably starting this Tuesday. When Fitzroy failed to recruit other Barnswell kids to fill the job, he'd find out how tough it was running a beach. Maybe no one had drowned in Chicopee in recent memory, but the potential was always there, especially when there was no supervision. Hotel guests would get nervous about leaving their kids on the beach. Maybe they'd decide not to stay at the Sherborne. Business would take a nosedive.

Face it, Fitzroy, Hunter thought smugly, I've got you by the balls.

At noon, as always, Hunter made his way into town. He usually joined Anabelle at Lord Michael's for a bite, but last night she'd called to ask if they could meet at the less crowded sandwich shop. It was quieter there, and she wanted to talk. Hunter could imagine. Poor Muffin was still lost, and why couldn't Hunter track down the girl he gave the cat to? Stupidly, he'd once said he thought he'd spotted Muffin by the lake. He had gone through the charade of crisscrossing the beach a half dozen times with Anabelle, calling out *kitty-kitty-kitty* in a falsetto voice. The way people had stared made him feel foolish and stupid. When was Anabelle going to give up?

"Hi," Hunter called, waving to Anabelle at a rear table. Her hair was swept back and tied with a barrette, a style he'd never seen her wear before, and for a change she wore makeup. She looked older. She was playing with the key around her neck, twisting the chain back and forth. He leaned over to kiss her.

"How was your morning? Okay? Did you meet with Fitzroy?" She asked so quickly it seemed she didn't really care.

"Some meeting. Fitzroy threatened to sack us if we don't work Tuesdays." Hunter lolled his head back, smiling in anticipation. "He doesn't know what he's in for. We're not going to be fired. We're going on strike . . ."

Anabelle said nothing and sat playing with her chain. Her lack of interest annoyed Hunter. "What's the matter?" he asked. Okay, the cat, he silently conceded, or some other dumb thing. He winked at Anabelle. "Hey, you know you look terrific. The hair style is stunning. Really."

"Hunter, please . . ."

"Please what? You're gorgeous."

"I don't want to hear that now."

He laughed. "Just paying you a compliment. There's nothing wrong with being the most beautiful creature—"

"Stop it!"

Hunter surrendered and let his eyes swim to the menu. What was bugging her? She'd been moody lately, keeping to herself. It was incredible the grief he had to take sometimes. Anabelle could really get on her high horse.

"Hunter, I've been wanting to tell you this for a while.

It's been hard for me. I don't know where to start . . . but . . . you and I . . ."

"What?" he said impatiently.

She took an exaggerated breath. "I think you and I should break up. At least for a while."

His body stiffened. An acrid, coppery taste flooded his mouth and thickened his tongue. "I didn't hear you."

"We need to be apart for a while."

"You're crazy."

"I'm serious."

He laughed awkwardly. "No, you're not."

"Don't threaten me. The way you just said that—it's like I'm not allowed to break up with you."

He eased back in his chair, trying to think things out. The shock made it hard. Why was she pulling this? Who put her up to it? "This is a game, isn't it?"

"No," she said in a small voice.

"What have I done—"

"Nothing. It has to do more with me than you."

"I don't believe this is happening," he muttered.

"I'm sorry, Hunter, I really am. I don't want to hurt you."

"Isn't this a little sudden? I mean, from out of nowhere you lay this on me?"

"It hasn't been sudden for me. It's been building. I should have told you sooner." She was standing up to him, unafraid, but then she must have felt sorry for him because she reached for his hand. "I love you. You know that. It's just that I don't want to spend all my time with you. I want more freedom. I need time and space."

"Freedom?" He made a twisted smile. It was all he could do not to sound cynical. "Time and space to do what?"

"I don't know. To be myself. To have fun."

"What are you talking about? We have fun together."

"On the surface maybe. But underneath you're always so serious. You're basically judgmental and you never seem really happy. When we're together I feel almost intimidated, I can't be myself. You sometimes even sound like my father. Like when we went skinny-dipping in the lake that night. I wanted to stay, but you couldn't wait to leave."

The panic had bunched at the bottom of Hunter's stomach, a cold, hard feeling that had nowhere to go. He felt lost and disoriented. Anabelle had said crazy things before, done crazy things, but nothing like this. Hunter ordered himself to be calm. He had to show her he was in control. She would come around. "Have you talked to your parents? To your father? They've always given you good advice."

"That's the whole point. How can I be independent if I run back to my parents all the time?"

"Then you and I'll talk about this," he said, trying to sound wise. "There's no point in being rash. We've been together too long. When we go out this Saturday. Just a quiet dinner. Plenty of time to work things out."

Her face hardened. The eyes became slits. "I can't go out with you Saturday."

"We have a date," he said firmly.

"I'm breaking it."

"Why? For whom?" He was losing control. The anger was like a flood, sweeping over him. "Who is he?" he demanded.

"It doesn't matter. No one special, I promise you. Even if there wasn't some new boy, I'd break our date. I want to date a lot of boys.

"Who is he?"

"None of your business. And you're missing the point."

Hunter shook his head, furious. Anabelle didn't understand. He cared for her. He only wanted what was best for her. "Tell me who," he demanded. When her face stayed blank he seized her wrist.

She pulled back, stunned. He was immediately sorry. He had blown it. She probably thought he was desperate.

Anabelle wanted to say something but instead, shook her head sadly and walked out. Hunter shut his eyes in despair. What was the point of following her? What was the point of doing anything? Everyone was ganging up. Fitzroy. Skip and Toby. Now Anabelle. They were trying to hurt him, ruin his life. What gratitude, after all he'd done for them.

The self-pity immobilized him like a poison. He ordered a hamburger but couldn't lift it to his mouth. Anabelle, I love you, he thought. You're mine, no one else's. And I'll get whoever thinks he'll take you from me.

An hour passed before he could pick himself up and head back to work.

CHAPTER 9

Reggie twisted up his face to the mirror, sloped the razor across his chin, and watched himself pull back in pain. He couldn't believe it. Third cut tonight. Steam billowed out from the shower and coated the mirror, but he could see the nick plainly. Drops of blood had seeped out to rest in the hollow above his chin. His new date would think he was Scarface.

Everyone was dressed but Max, who continued to croon in the shower, mixing up old Beatles' songs. Reggie stuck a shred of toilet paper to his latest wound and quickly ducked out of the latrine. The steam had turned his shirt into random dark patches that clung to his ribs. He minded, but not terribly. To have hot water finally was worth some minor discomforts. After a million requests to the hotel to fix their water heater, Max had examined the copper pipes himself, spotted the rusted couplings, and with tools borrowed from the hotel's maintenance shop he worked the magic of a plumber's son. That act alone had made him a hero. Arranging tonight's beach party only put him on a higher pedestal.

Reggie grabbed one of the beers that Tiny had picked up for the party. He needed the courage, he thought, swallowing easily. As his eyes darted around the room he couldn't believe Philip. Everyone else was dressed in jeans and sport shirts, while Philip looked like he was going to a yacht club.

Philip's final touch was cologne. Reggie wanted to hold his nose, but instead he smiled.

"Looking pretty sharp," said Reggie.

Philip nodded presumptuously, as if of course he looked great. "Just for the record, folks," he announced, "I've got dibs on the redhead tonight. The one Max claims has nice legs."

"You should see her braces," said Tiny.

"Hey, seriously." Philip's arrogant voice cut through the laughter. "She's mine, okay? Redheads and I are famous for getting along. Runs in the family."

"Whatever you say, Philip," Tiny added, "except I think Kenny's got his eye on her, too."

Kenny shrugged self-consciously at the joke and wandered outside. Reggie felt for him. Kenny didn't really want to come tonight, Reggie guessed, but he couldn't fight the momentum of the cabin. A color photo of his girl was Scotch-taped to the inside of his footlocker, a blond who looked every inch as wholesome and unimaginative as Kenny. The photo was like an icon to him, something to worship before bed every night. Reggie could almost feel the guilt welling up in Kenny. Just to anticipate partying with another girl probably meant betrayal.

"I'll take anything," Washington put in, "as long as she's got a skirt." The giraffelike neck twisted slowly around the room. "Hey, what about you, Reggie?"

"Max already picked one out for me," he answered. "She's supposed to be cute. Brown eyes, short hair, a Debra Winger smile . . ." He was afraid that his tone was too serious, and that everyone would jump on him. Thinking over what Max had said the other night, Reggie had decided he should go to the party. Maybe he did need to loosen up, get back in the swing of things, like his mom had always said. The problem was he'd never dated much, even before his dad's death. Girls made him uneasy. He didn't have a gift for delivering smooth lines like Max did, or even Tiny's humor, so every word was slow and deliberate. Painful. Weather, the high school football team, a new movie in town—he wasn't a great conversationalist. He worried that girls might think he was a loser. Girls could talk, he knew, and word got around.

"She sounds okay, Reggie," said Tiny. "You're going to have a ball tonight. I'll let you in on a secret . . ."

"What?"

"If your girl's a real cutie, let her know she's got a fabulous brain too.Tell her she's another Einstein."

"Why?" he couldn't help asking.

"Because good-looking chicks are insecure about their intelligence. And vice versa. If a girl is brainy, you have to tell her she looks like a million, even if she's got the face of a horny toad. She'll love you forever."

"Come off it," Philip sneered. He seemed amused by the theory. "You want to snow a chick? You act totally casual. Almost bored. Like she doesn't mean anything to you. You're not rude, but you're hardly excited. Make her think something's wrong, and that it's her fault. The next thing you know, she's got her paws all over you."

"Maybe that works for you preppies," Washington countered, "but it's not the dude's way. The dude romances his lady. The dude treats her like a queen. Spends bread on her. Reads poetry. Whispers sweet nothings in her ear . . ."

Incredible, thought Reggie. All of a sudden everyone was a swinger. Earlier, there were doubts about having a party at all. Max might have done a snow job on Anabelle, Tiny pointed out, but what was to guarantee that her girlfriends would flip over the rest of them? They were just summer help, out-of-town waiters. Max had gotten a good laugh. What a bunch of sheep, he said. Didn't anyone realize that Barnswell girls were bored out of their skulls? They wanted a change. Barnswell boys were old hat. Besides, this was just one party—what was the big deal?

"Show time!" a voice boomed. Max was tucking in his shirt as he marched into the room. Reggie had never seen him any slicker, not like Philip, but looking like a magazine model in his faded jeans and blue work shirt. He motioned to Tiny and Washington to grab the beer. "Okay, it's almost ten-thirty. We rendezvous with the ladies at eleven, about a mile down from the hotel beach. No partying till we get there. After turning off the cabin lights we walk out very quietly, avoid the hotel security, and head along the shore road. Someone has to drop into town on the way. The bartender at Lord Michael's is going to slip us a couple bottles of Scotch."

"Scotch? Who needs Scotch?" Tiny complained. "We've got enough beer for the Fifth Army."

Max wagged his head in disappointment. "Scotch happens to be a class drink, and these are class ladies. Now who wants to go?"

When there were no volunteers Max's eyes circled the room. "I already paid for the booze. All you do is ask for Steve. He'll put everything in a brown paper bag." His gaze stopped on Reggie. "Harrison, how about you?" It was more of a command than a request.

"I don't know . . ."

"You can remember the name *Steve*, can't you?"

Reggie looked at him reluctantly. While the errand was probably no big deal, he could forsee problems. What if someone from the hotel staff was at the pub? Or maybe Reggie would get carded, and when they found he was under age the police might be called. Or the bartender could claim he hadn't gotten paid. A lot of possibilities.

"Hey, Harrison, it's no big deal," Max said, as if reading his mind.

"Okay," Reggie said after a moment. Max was right. He was sweating things too much.

"If you don't show up at the beach in a while, I'll come looking for you," Max promised.

Reggie walked with the others alongside a row of guest cottages, out of sight of the night watchman, and exited on the shore road. Max kidded Reggie about not running off with the Scotch, then he and the others forked off toward the beach. Reggie propped himself against a tree and tried to relax. The town glittered before him. Distant voices, spontaneous and full of life, broke the silence that was the hotel's. Max was right. The Sherborne resembled a prison.

He found Lord Michael's without any trouble and slipped through the door. No one asked him about an ID. The place smelled of pizza. A jukebox blasted away, and the dance floor was mobbed with well-dressed kids. Reggie glanced at his own clothes and weaved quietly to the bar. He asked the bartender if his name was Steve. The college-age boy shook his head. Steve was away. But he'd be back in twenty minutes.

Reggie debated whether to ask for the booze anyway. No, better to wait. Less chance of trouble. Pulling a dollar from his pocket he ordered a beer, drank it quickly, and then a second. He had started on his third when the noise erupted from the doorway. He glanced over, groaning to himself as he recognized the lifeguards. Led by Anabelle's boyfriend, they pushed their way toward the bar, backslapping friends on the way. They crossed into the empty space next to him.

Great, Reggie thought, wonderful. Just what he needed. Arms reached over his shoulder for mugs of beer. Bodies stumbled into his stool. He tried to shift away but it was impossible. He couldn't decide exactly what to do. Should he slip out quietly, or stay and wait for Steve? The wait couldn't be much longer. Max would be disappointed, maybe even annoyed, if he didn't bring back the liquor. He didn't even know exactly why, but he wanted to please Max.

Reggie turned at a right angle from the bar, trying to ignore the lifeguards. He watched Hunter. Obviously this guy was drunk and out of control. One moment Hunter was yelling good-naturedly to friends in the pub, and the next he was grumbling to himself. His pals crowded around, trying to cheer him up, but it didn't work. Reggie looked at his watch.

"Hey—what . . . who spilled . . ." a voice flared in anger.

Confused, Reggie twisted around to discover the knocked over mug. A river of beer had eddied onto Hunter and soaked his jeans. Reggie's beer. He felt a flush of panic. Not thinking, he picked up the mug and set it right.

"Was that yours, klutz?" Hunter demanded of Reggie, as he blotted up the beer on his jeans.

No, Reggie thought, but he knew it was. What he meant was he hadn't knocked it over. All those reaching arms and elbows. Reggie wagged his head and looked away.

"Hey, I'm talking to you, meathead."

Reggie felt a pit opening in his stomach. His hands were sweating.

"Meathead—"

"I'm sorry," he said, still afraid to look at Hunter.

"You're *sorry?*"

He apologized again, but it was as if Hunter didn't hear.

Reggie knew he was doomed. An apology wasn't enough. Hunter was too proud. The other lifeguards had stopped talking to focus on Reggie.

"You're one of the waiters at the Sherborne," someone said. "You play water polo at the beach . . ."

"Hey, what do you know?" Hunter chimed in, studying Reggie more carefully. A thin, knowing smile came to his lips. "You're friends with the big monkey, the one who was looking Anabelle over at the restaurant."

Reggie was quiet.

"Aren't you?" Hunter insisted.

"I don't know what you're talking about," he said quietly.

"And here it is, eleven o'clock," Hunter went on. "Curfew for hotel waiters. Only you're sitting at our bar—"

"I'm not a waiter," Reggie said in a scratchy voice. Stupid. Really dumb. What else was it? Dressed like he was, no one would think he was a tourist, and he certainly wasn't from Barnswell.

Hunter laughed oddly and turned to his friends. "What do you think of liars, Skip?"

"Not much."

"Hey, Hunter, lay off the kid," another boy said.

"I'm not bugging him, am I? I just want to ask a couple questions. What's your name, kid?"

Play along, thought Reggie. Be nice and everything might work out. Besides, he was good at being polite. "Reggie."

"How do you do, Reggie. My name's Hunter Braxton." A hand was extended and Reggie shook it. "Now tell me, Reggie, about your fellow waiter. The big gorilla. What's his name?"

He hesitated. "Max."

"Max," Hunter repeated for his audience. "Some name. He's your friend?"

Reggie shrugged. "Sure."

"A good friend?"

"Yeah."

"Where is he?" asked Hunter.

"What?"

"What's Max doing tonight?"

"I don't know." Reggie could hardly breathe. No more questions, he thought. He didn't want trouble.

"Hey, Reggie, I think you're lying to us again. I think you're covering up." Hunter's face had turned impatient. "Because *I* know where Max is. He's with my girl. He's Anabelle's date tonight. *Isn't he?*"

Anger flashed through Reggie. Where was Steve? No, where was Max? He'd promised to come if Reggie didn't show at the party. Reggie was sticking his neck out for the cabin, and now, when he needed help . . . "No," Reggie said, forcing out the words, "I don't think Max even knows your girlfriend."

Without warning the pain started on the nape of his neck. A deep, fierce scalding that spiraled downward. He jerked away, writhing, to shake loose whatever was on him. The roar of laughter filled his ears. Reggie thrust a hand to his back to put out the flames. He felt like a clown, but he was in agony.

Slowly, the pain began to ease. Hunter looked at Reggie with his thin, wise-ass smile, holding up the empty pizza tray. "Oh, my, how clumsy of me," he chided himself. "So sorry, Reggie the Liar."

The pizza lumps in his shirt were starting to harden. He was still breathing rapidly, out of control, too humiliated to speak. The urge to cry began to build. He pushed away from the bar and stumbled outside. When he was alone, he shook out the gobs of pizza. He felt hopeless and defeated. He was a first-class idiot. Why had he ever agreed to go to the pub? It was asking for trouble. A chance he didn't have to take.

He drifted along the shore road. Cars passed him in blurs, their headlights sweeping over the asphalt. In the distance, near the lake, he finally spotted a bonfire. Through the mixture of shrieks and radio music he could hear Max, the booming voice holding court, and in the lulls there were softer voices, girlish laughter. Dancing couples were silhouetted by the fire, led by Tiny's paunchy figure. Washington moved his arms like a professional dancer. As Reggie approached, Kenny Homer jumped up with a slanty grin. Was it really Kenny? The dull, complacent eyes had expanded into greenish lagoons, and the wet, patted down hair looked demonic. His breath was foul. "Com'n join ush, Reg," he said.

Reggie smiled indifferently and squatted by the fire, flattening his hands out for warmth. His eyes wandered to Max and Anabelle. They had their arms around each other with an almost comical passion, like two long-lost lovers. He might have laughed if he'd been in the mood. When Max finally looked up he waved to Reggie.

"Where've you been?" he called out. "Let's open that Scotch. I've got ice and cups—"

"I didn't get it," Reggie said.

"What? What the hell happened?"

"You don't want to know."

"Come on, tell me." He excused himself from Anabelle and crawled over. "We've been waiting almost an hour," Max said, lowering his voice. "Your girl gave up on you and went home. She was really pissed, Reggie. Didn't look good for the cabin . . ."

"I'm broken up." Reggie tried to calm down. Finally he

told Max everything. About waiting for the bartender. Hunter and his buddies showing up. The hostile questions. Hot pizza being dumped down his shirt. "I thought you were going to come looking for me," he said when he finished.

"I was going to."

"But you were too busy, right?" Reggie glanced disapprovingly at Anabelle. "Sure."

"Hey, I'm sorry."

"That's what Hunter said. 'So Sorry, Reggie the Liar.' " He shivered at the memory. "You know, I went out on a limb for you. I didn't tell him you were with Anabelle tonight." He was still upset, spitting out the words. How could he have ever considered Max a potential friend? Max was always so self-absorbed, as if he didn't really care about anyone else. Frustrated, Reggie picked himself up and headed down the beach.

"Hey, where are you going?" Max shouted after him.

Reggie didn't turn, he'd had enough. Max and the others could do what they liked, but for the rest of the summer Reggie would stick around the hotel. No more taking risks. Suddenly he heard footsteps and felt Max's hand on his shoulder.

"Just hold on, will you?" Max swept the hair out of his eyes as he caught his breath. "Look, you probably think I'm a real rat for not looking for you. Okay—you're right."

"Tell me about it," said Reggie.

"I was selfish. I should have gone for the booze myself. You're a nice guy. I figured you'd understand, I wanted to be with Anabelle."

Reggie said nothing, bowing his head as he plodded along. Max grew frustrated as he tried to keep up.

"Reggie, listen to me, will you please? I'll make it up to you. Promise. You want me to, I can tell by your face. I will.

You want me to leave Anabelle and find your date for you? Wait here—"

"No thanks."

"Come on—"

"Maybe I don't want the date, did you ever think of that?"

"Then what do you want me to do? Say it—anything. I'd like to be your friend—listen, we both need friends . . ."

"There's nothing you can do. Just leave me alone. Let's forget the evening ever happened."

Reggie spun away, leaving a perplexed Max behind. Maybe Max really was sorry, Reggie conceded, but he wasn't in the mood to be consoled. As he walked he studied the gentle lapping of the water on the sand and an occasional stick that had been washed ashore. He kicked at one disinterestedly, then he spotted a dark, furish lump, half in the water. Bending over, he touched the strange object with his finger. His stomach tightened. It was an animal. The brown and gold kitten's eyes were open and grotesquely bloated. The tongue stuck out like a flattened eraser tip. Only the long tail, curled up, looked normal. The smell suddenly hit him and he pulled back.

The cat had to have been dead for several days at least, maybe weeks. The lake had finally surrendered it. Reggie wondered how it had drowned. The mystery saddened him. With his hands he dug a deep hole in the sand, pushed the cat in gently with his foot, and covered over the grave.

His stomach was still reeling as he moved on. It was only a cat, but he was shook. The death was premature, and so horrible. He remembered his father's funeral, how helpless and angry he'd felt. As the casket was lowered into the roughly dug hole, he'd stared out blankly, in shock. No, it couldn't be, he had thought, he couldn't let it be. There was no such thing as death. But then the dirt had been shoveled on top, to prove him wrong. His heart pounded wildly.

A wind lifted silently off the lake. Reggie dropped his head and plodded along. Pull yourself together, he thought. Your father's dead. You have to forget him. But he felt a quiver inside him, where the terror and sadness still gathered, like a cold spot that would never warm.

CHAPTER 10

"Our lunch specials for Wednesday are lobster salad, Quiche Lorraine, Chicken Kiev, and—if I may offer my own recommendation—braised short ribs." Max maintained his polished smile as the two women made up their minds. As always he looked poised and sure of himself, but his stomach was churning. One eye kept jumping to the neighboring table where Fitzroy and Carlton were gorging themselves. When would the food manager leave? Max needed to speak to Fitzroy alone.

"The lobster salad, please," the woman with the butterfly-frame glasses said.

Her companion squinted in indecision. "I suppose the same, if you promise us it's fresh. And you won't forget the lemon wedges—"

Max nodded dutifully, ready to please, but he'd already sized up the two as a lost cause. Instinct told him they were non-tippers. Too fussy. It was galling to him how stingy the wealthy could sometimes be, and how much they took for granted. Despite his charm, Max found that his tips were getting smaller and less frequent. A third of the season was gone and he'd saved nowhere near his goal. He had begun to worry until he had his brainstorm, for which he had to thank Anabelle for the inspiration. He was crazy about her anyway, but after what she'd revealed about Hunter at the party, he loved her even more.

"Mr. Fitzroy," Max called, as the hotel manager started to leave. Max caught up with him near the lobby. Carlton was a step behind like a clinging shadow. Too bad, thought Max, but he had to make his move. Timing was critical. He only wished he knew more about Fitzroy than what he'd read in the hotel brochure.

"Young man?" Fitzroy turned slowly, half bracing himself against the wall.

"Sir, my name's Max Riley. I've been your waiter from time to time."

"Of course. A good waiter, too."

"Thank you, sir. It's been a pleasure serving you. Always an honor serving a fellow countryman . . ."

Fitzroy edged closer to study the handsome Irish face. Very slowly, a crease of approval came to his lips. "Max *Riley?*" he repeated.

"Yes, sir. My grandfather came from Dublin."

"Dublin, is it?"

"A lovely city, sir," Max said, though he knew nothing about it. "My absolute favorite."

"You know, my mother was a Dubliner . . . rest her soul."

"I didn't know you had ties there, sir."

"Oh, yes," he said wistfully. "Have you ever visited—"

"Just once, when I was a kid."

"Wonderful. Are you enjoying working at the hotel?"

Max hesitated. "That's what I wanted to talk to you about, sir."

Carlton cocked his head suspiciously. "If you're having a problem with your job," he spoke up, "you talk to me, Mr. Riley. That's procedure."

"It's not exactly my job," Max said, turning to Fitzroy. "It's about another job. I was thinking of the lifeguards, sir. I noticed their towers were vacant this morning, and then I heard rumors about a strike."

"Those boys may think they're on a strike," Fitzroy answered huffily, "but they're really being fired."

"Terrible thing to happen," Max ventured. "To the hotel, I mean. I was wondering, Mr. Fitzroy, if you'd found anyone to replace them."

"There'll be an ad in the evening paper."

"But you haven't found anyone yet." Max felt relief when Fitzroy shook his head ruefully. "Sir, have you perhaps considered using some of us in the hotel as lifeguards?"

"Us?" Carlton interrupted. The eyelids batted uncontrollably. "Who is 'us'?"

"Frankly, our cabin wants to offer its services, even on a short-term basis. We're all good swimmers. It might be a week or more before the hotel finds replacements from town." All Max wanted was a foot in the door. Once he was on the beach, he was confident of finding a way to stay. "In the meantime, you don't want a beach without lifeguards—"

"I think we're aware of our risks," Carlton said as he stepped between Max and Fitzroy. "And I don't believe it's a waiter's position to suggest solutions. In any event, your idea hasn't much merit."

"Why not?" Max asked boldly.

"We need you as waiters. The hotel can't afford to play musical chairs with its help."

"Let's not be hasty." Fitzroy, troubled, looked at his friend. "We have enough kitchen help to spare for our dining rooms. It's easier to find waiters. The beach is important. If these boys can swim—why not?"

"Because the hotel has always hired its lifeguards from Barnswell. It's a tradition," Carlton said distinctly.

"Some tradition," Fitzroy complained. "Look where it's gotten us. Those rapscallions—"

"There's another consideration," Carlton interjected. "The Sherborne requires its lifeguards to be certified by the Red Cross." He smiled at Max. "Are you certified?"

Max hesitated, sorry for the answer he was about to give. "No, sir."

"Too bad," Carlton commiserated.

"But I'm willing to take the test. We all are. Under the pressing circumstances," Max continued, "maybe the hotel could give us its own test."

"I don't think that's possible," Carlton said coolly.

"We're very eager to help."

"Très bien, très bien," Fitzroy interrupted, motioning that he had to go. *"C'est possible. Peut-être. Peut-être . . ."*

Max watched them march off, not sure what the hotel manager had said, but he was hopeful. The overriding fact was that the hotel was desperate; it needed replacements in a hurry. Max had taken a few liberties in his plea to Fitzroy. He had yet to broach the lifeguard jobs with anyone in the cabin, but he was sure it would be an easy sell. To laze around in a tower all day, soaking up rays, watching girls parade by . . .

No one wanted the job more than Max. Not only would he earn better money and make his life easier, he'd have more time with Anabelle. If he could have his way, they'd be together every night. So far it was frustrating. For whatever reason, Anabelle was evasive. *Maybe* she'd go out with him again. *Maybe* they could meet for lunch. *Maybe* they'd take an outboard for a spin on the lake. Was she serious or not? He knew *he* was serious but he wasn't sure about Anabelle.

When he'd asked about the key around her neck, at first

she told him it belonged to a friend, then Hunter, until she finally admitted it just opened a back door to her house. She came and went pretty much as she pleased. Anabelle said proudly that she didn't worry about her parents' approval. Max looked hard at the gold chain and asked her what it would take to get it off her neck. She only laughed, and at that moment he realized not only was Anabelle someone he wanted, she was someone he couldn't be without.

After the party Max had walked Anabelle home. He kissed her good night and waited till she was inside. But he didn't leave. When her footsteps drifted up the stairs, he sneaked around the house, gingerly stepping over flowers as he spied in. Her home was magnificent. He thought of his own family's dumpy little tract house in Bradley, something a good wind would knock a hole through. To Max's everlasting surprise, his folks seemed content. They'd waited twenty years to pay off the mortgage, and now that the house was owned free and clear they wanted little more. That was their dream. Some dream, Max thought, uncomprehending. He sometimes asked why they never took a trip or bought an expensive car, and in reply their faces showed confusion. "You think money grows on trees, Max?" his father would answer. "I'm a plumber. Your mom and I are doing just fine. We're happy. Don't worry about us. Aren't you happy?"

Max didn't answer. He supposed he could see his father's point. Maybe his folks really were happy, and that was great. What upset Max was his mom and dad didn't understand *his* ambition, that *he* couldn't be happy until he'd made his mark on the world. He felt no shame in being a plumber's son—after all, he loved his parents—and he'd told his dad that over and over. Max accepted what he was, but that didn't mean, given a fair shake, he couldn't improve his lot. What was so wrong with wanting to make money? Money did a lot to ease life's bumps and jolts. More vacations, more things to buy. You didn't worry about losing your job. You didn't even *need* a job. Not only that, Max thought, it seemed that automatically other people looked up to you. Anabelle and her family were prime examples.

Max finished his work in the kitchen, washed up, and hurried back to the cabin. Everyone was lounging around. Reggie was glued to another paperback and barely glanced up as Max sauntered in.

"Isn't this a great day?" Max called out good-naturedly. A smile inched up his face.

"What's so great about it? My back's killing me," moaned Washington. He limped toward the john. "Those trays get heavier every day."

"Maybe you need a vacation," Max suggested.

"Sure," Tiny piped, "and don't forget the gold Mercedes."

"Hey, Tiny, come here." Max pointed out the cabin window to the beach. Girls in bikinis were jogging by the lake's edge. Water-skiers crisscrossed Chicopee in lazy arcs. "Isn't that a gorgeous sight? A lot prettier than the Sherborne dining room?"

"Yeah, gorgeous," Kenny said, coming over. "So what?"

"I mean, wouldn't you guys rather be down there, near the water, than up here?"

Philip smirked. "Would I rather be the king of England than the Hunchback of Notre Dame?"

"Exactly, Philip. And I have a way."

Max stripped off his shirt, playfully flexed his biceps like he was Arnold Schwarzenegger, and explained his new plan.

CHAPTER 11

"Us?" Tiny exclaimed. "We're going to be lifeguards?"

"Us," Max affirmed.

"Alll-rrrright . . ." Philip shouted, slapping hands with Kenny and Washington. "Give me my whistle and I'll climb into my tower!"

"Who did you talk to?" Kenny asked Max.

"The head honcho—Fitzroy. He was going to think about it, but my hunch is we're in. All we have to do probably is pass a dumb swimming test."

"Uh oh," Washington said, frowning. "I can barely dog paddle."

"You'll be okay," Max assured him, and then he turned to Reggie. "Hey, what do you think?" he called out.

Reggie lifted his head slowly from his book, as if he'd already deliberated on an answer. "I'm not going to do it."

"What?" Max said playfully, cupping a hand behind his ear.

"You heard me. I'm not going to be a lifeguard."

Max didn't want to give up on Reggie. He found him a challenge. Max had already acknowledged that the incident at the pub was his fault. It wasn't right to let Reggie take abuse that was meant for him. But Max had figured that the lifeguard job would make up for that mistake. A real cushy way to spend the rest of the summer. Only Reggie was more stubborn than Max anticipated.

"Party pooper," Tiny said to Reggie. "Martyr."

Kenny threw his hands up. "You're whacko, Reg."

"No, let him alone," Max said, keeping the peace. "He doesn't have to if he doesn't want to. They're only five lifeguard positions."

"I still think he's nuts," Philip said.

"You guys are the ones who're crazy." Reggie swung his legs off the bunk and sat up. "Replacing those lifeguards is going to be nothing but trouble."

"Why?" demanded Tiny. "How can it possibly be trouble?"

"You're taking away Big Man Hunter's job. He'll get back at you. The guy's the Prince of Darkness."

"Wait a sec," Max interrupted. "Hunter may have a beef with me, but not with anyone else. We didn't force him to go on strike, did we? That's his problem. We're just helping out the hotel. I promise you that Hunter isn't going to bother anybody." Max made sure everyone heard. "The boy's all mouth and no action."

Everyone cheered.

"Keep dreaming," Reggie broke in, his voice struggling above the clamor like a stubborn and isolated philosopher.

"Harrison," Philip said, "you're nothing but a pantywaist. Just because the guy dumps a little pizza down your shirt it's not the end of the universe. Hunter isn't such a bad guy. Under other circumstances, we might all be friends."

"I know why Reggie won't be a lifeguard," Tiny observed. "Doesn't want the public to check out his body."

Philip gave a smirk. "Yeah, too skinny, and he's got muscles like a ten-year-old."

Max watched as Reggie recoiled from the laughter, his face crimsoning over as he left the cabin. No one seemed to care about his feelings. A few more jokes were exchanged as everyone put on swim trunks for the beach. Max went after Reggie.

"Let the wimp go," Philip shouted from the door. "Who needs him anyway?"

Max caught up with Reggie at the service entrance to the kitchen. He was still upset, his breathing coming in exaggerated spurts, and his hands were shaking. "Don't listen to them," Max said. "They're full of it."

"You sure you know what you're saying?" Reggie answered sarcastically. "They're your good buddies."

"You think so?"

"They worship you, don't they? They do exactly what you want. You're their leader."

"For now," Max allowed. "Tomorrow, who knows? I mean, you think I trust those guys? You think they'll always be loyal?"

Reggie seemed confused. He took a calming breath. "What do you mean?"

"Those goofuses don't have any character. They're okay, they're nice, and I like them, but they're part of the herd. They don't have guts, they don't have ambition. But you're different, Harrison. You stood up to Hunter. Just now you stood up to everyone in the cabin, including me. I admire you."

"You're just saying that," Reggie offered, half turning away.

"Harrison, I'm as sincere as I've ever been." Max meant it. Not that he was a perfect human being. He knew he was capable of being coldly opportunistic when the moment was right—but he had a heart too. He wanted Reggie to know that. "Hey, what the hell are you doing in the kitchen anyway? It's our time off."

"It's my turn to wax the dining room floor."

"By yourself?"

"Yeah," Reggie admitted, suddenly laughing. "Thrilling, isn't it?"

"Can't let you do that alone, Harrison," said Max. "It wouldn't be right." Max threw an arm around his shoulder. "Besides, what are friends for?"

Late that afternoon, as everyone dressed for the dinner shift, a hotel clerk appeared at the cabin. The envelope in his hand was embossed with the Sherborne seal, and Fitzroy's name was printed in fancy gold letters in the upper left-hand corner. Max opened the envelope carefully as the others clustered around.

Dear Mr. Riley:

On behalf of the hotel management, I wish to thank you for offering your cabin's services as lifeguards for the beach. It is my decision to take you up on your offer. Your salaries will match the regular lifeguards, prorated to your starting date. Please have everyone report to my office punctually at eight A.M. *tomorrow so we may discuss details.*

Sincerely,

R. Kennedy Fitzroy
Sherborne Manager

P.S. In what part of Dublin did your grandfather live?

Max howled in triumph. "Party time tonight!" he roared. Amidst the wild cheering, Tiny jumped on his bunk, as if it were a trampoline, and promptly broke through the slats holding the mattress. Everyone rejoiced but Reggie. Max noticed him sitting silently on his bed. Still doubting the wisdom of our triumph? Max wondered. This guy was something else.

CHAPTER 12

"How's the weather up there?"

Anabelle shielded her eyes and looked up to the tower as she spoke. Max and his friends had been lifeguards only a couple of days, but they acted like veterans, and almost everybody thought they were as conscientious as the old lifeguards. The strike had become a joke. Anabelle actually felt sorry for Hunter. She knew he must have felt betrayed by the hotel, but she hadn't seen him to commiserate. It was like him to hole up when he got angry. Skip and Toby hadn't seen him recently either.

"Anabelle, is that really you?" Max said, opening his arms with a mock flourish. He jumped from the tower. "I thought you'd gotten tired of me. I've been calling every night."

"I know. I guess I owe you an apology." She grabbed the whistle around his neck playfully. "I've been avoiding you since the party. I don't know why. Can I make it up to you and take you to lunch?"

"You want to take me? What about if I take you?"

"That makes you sound insecure," she teased. "Can't a girl ask a boy?"

"Okay, take me to lunch. I'll be off duty in an hour."

"I was thinking of tomorrow."

"What's wrong with the here and now?"

"Nothing, except I'm supposed to go shopping with Mom." Max looked disappointed, she noticed, but he didn't pout, not like Hunter sometimes did. "Tomorrow, okay?" she said, and she let Max kiss her cheek good-bye. She liked him, she thought, as she headed up to the road, but how much she wasn't sure. He was so different from Hunter and the other boys she'd known. Hunter was plodding and predictable while Max was so spontaneous and fun. The way he pranced around the beach, twirling his whistle lanyard around his finger, cocky and nonchalant. The way he pursued her. Max seemed so sure of himself.

Sometimes she just wanted to give in to him, but another voice told her to be careful. The problem, she'd decided, was there were really two Anabelles. The one who was always good and did what was expected of her, and the new one who wanted to explore and try new things. She'd tried to explain to Hunter what she was going through, hoping for some sympathy, but she'd failed miserably. He laughed when she talked about being independent. He didn't understand what she was saying or feeling. She knew she was changing but she wasn't sure how. Sometimes it scared her but there was no turning back. Becoming her own person might mean leaving behind things and people she cared about, but more than anything she needed to grow up.

Only it was more difficult each day. After the beach party, she told herself she'd drunk too much beer, gone too far with Max, made a fool of herself. Where was her self-respect? Max kept calling for a second date but she was afraid to say yes. Anabelle had never gone seriously with anyone but Hunter. The thought of a new boy in her life was thrilling, but it made her anxious, too.

Walking along the shore road, Anabelle's thoughts were interrupted when she heard her name called. She peeked around. The beach sparkled under the exploding sun. Then she spotted Hunter, alone, a short way down the road.

"Where have you been?" she asked, concerned. He looked glassy-eyed and unkempt.

"Who cares? You writing my biography?"

"Come on, Hunter—"

"We have to talk," he said. It was almost an order.

"About what?"

"—things."

"Exactly what?" she asked, though she could guess. She ran a finger nervously through her hair. She didn't feel like dealing with him right now. "I don't have time. We'll talk later."

"You mean you have no time for me at all." He laughed bitterly as he watched Anabelle glancing out to the beach. "Why don't you wave to your new boyfriend? He's king of the mountain now."

She sighed. "Okay, I like Max. So what? I would like him no matter how things had turned out for you." She wanted Hunter to know that. She said it genuinely.

"Sure, tell me about it. He takes my girl, then my job. Skip and Toby are pissed at me. The rest of the town is laughing."

"I still like you, Hunter," she said, wanting him to feel better. And it was true. Maybe they'd even get back together, if Hunter would stop being so possessive. The more jealous he got, the more freedom she wanted, but he didn't understand.

"You think I'm the lowest form of human life," he said suddenly.

"That's not true. How do you know what I'm thinking?"

"I know," he said.

"You're just feeling sorry for yourself. And what bothers me even more is that you take Max so seriously. Like he's your sworn enemy."

His face contorted. "What do you think he is—my new best friend?"

"Why can't I like you both?" she protested.

"Because you can't. If you're falling for him, there's no room for me. It's either one or the other."

"That's sounds ridiculous," she said, and started to walk away. Hunter followed, still fuming.

"Do you know anything about that creep?" he asked. "I checked up on him. He goes to a public school. His dad has a plumbing shop. Is that the kind of guy you're attracted to? Come on, Anabelle."

"What difference does his background make?" she asked.

"It shows you've got nothing in common. For chrissake, Anabelle, one of your ancestors signed the Declaration of Independence."

She was amused. Hunter thought her family history was special, but she hated when anyone used it as if it could make her different—better. She suddenly liked the thought that Max wasn't rich or socially prominent.

"Have you told your father about Max?" Hunter asked.

"Don't play games. You told him yourself." That move had made Anabelle angry. Hunter had called several times immediately after the beach party, and when her father answered Hunter tried to line up her parents against Max. Daddy took Hunter's side. Anabelle resented it. Just because her father was an Andover alumnus, and he and Hunter's dad belonged to the Princeton Club, her father felt that they deserved loyalty. Who cared about that stuff anyway? What about loyalty to his daughter's feelings?

The more her parents argued in Hunter's favor, the more Anabelle wanted to see Max. Why couldn't they just back off for a while? Her parents were always afraid that she wouldn't make the "correct" decisions about life: where to go to college, who to marry, when to have babies. Babies! No one in her family knew how to have a good time *now*. She wasn't even seventeen yet.

"I don't think we should talk anymore," Anabelle said to Hunter suddenly. "This is getting unpleasant."

"Oh, I see. I'm making you uncomfortable. So sorry. You wouldn't have any idea how I feel, would you?"

"Just go away, please."

"I hope you know everybody's disappointed in you. This hick pulls a number, and you fall for it. I thought you had some brains—"

"Stop it!"

"Or is this another of Anabelle's little games? Just like your precious kitten—one minute you're grief stricken, and the next you've forgotten you ever had a cat. Right now you've got a crush on that ape, but in a couple of weeks it'll be someone else, to prove you're independent. Ha! You'll be back doing just what your parents want as soon as you get in trouble and need their help."

"Are you quite finished now?"

"I've just started."

"I'm walking home," Anabelle said firmly. "I don't want you to follow me. Do you understand?"

To her surprise, Hunter stayed at the corner. Anabelle was almost in tears. Hunter had made her furious.

"You better break up with the goofball," he suddenly called out. "Or else—"

She wasn't going to answer. He wouldn't intimidate her, no matter what he said. But as she moved more quickly his voice caught up with her again, a thin, cold knife of a voice that made her shiver.

"You're not going to do this to me, Anabelle! No way in the world! I'm tougher and smarter and I won't lose!"

CHAPTER 13

The sun, always the mighty sun.

In his tower, Reggie squinted out at the mad scene. Like wandering nomads, hotel guests were toting chairs, umbrellas, flotation tubes, buckets and shovels. They stumbled into one another, spilled food, drenched themselves in suntan oil. Chaos.

Reggie had his own problem to distract him. Whenever he pressed a finger into his thighs, reddish blotches appeared. By evening his legs would be fried, in spite of the lotion he'd put on. He wondered if mosquitoes liked well-done flesh. What an oddball he was. His burned face and legs contrasted with the crisply tanned bodies that stretched between him and the lake, and he imagined he was the scrawniest lifeguard in the history of Barnswell. How had he let Max talk him into this? When Washington failed the hotel swimming test for the second time, Reggie had no choice. "You have to join us," Max said. "I promised Fitzroy five guards. If we don't come through we could be sent back to the kitchen. All of us. You don't want to let the cabin down, do you?"

Reggie didn't really care about the others, but Max was hard to fight. He had given Reggie a silent message that what Reggie did was really important to him. Thinking everything over, Reggie knew he couldn't let Max down. Max *needed* the lifeguard job. It was more than the money, or Anabelle, or the triumph of acing out Hunter. It was as if Max's destiny were on the line.

To his surprise, Reggie found he was rather happy with the new beach job. He didn't miss Carlton's benign despot presence every morning, nor scurrying around with twenty-five pound trays on his shoulder. Lifeguarding was a comparative piece of cake. As long as Hunter and his pals didn't show up . . . When Reggie got bored and wanted to be entertained, he turned to Max. Before, as waiters, when they'd played water polo, Max had mimicked Hunter mercilessly; now Max was the ham, plugging his whistle in his mouth continually to make his presence known. Reggie enjoyed the show. And when it came to drama, Reggie himself had held center stage briefly. His third day on the job he'd rescued an eight-year-old girl with leg cramps who was floundering. Half the beach had swarmed around them, awed by Reggie's heroism. Bewildered, he'd clambered silently back into his tower. What was the big deal? He hadn't exactly been in danger. It was his job, wasn't it? He realized some of the other boys might have made a production out of it, but that wasn't Reggie's style. Better just to be left alone.

"Hey, what time is it?" Reggie yelled across the beach to Max. The growling in his stomach was slowly becoming a roar. He and Max always took the first lunch break at noon, while the others went at one. Max didn't answer. He was too busy waving at Anabelle, who looked spectacular as she approached in a two-piece bathing suit, her blond hair falling softly on her shoulders, and the dark glasses hiked up on her forehead. A genuine "10," Reggie had to admit. But her beauty didn't mean anything to him. He climbed down his tower, disappointed. Whenever Anabelle showed up, which was often, lunch plans got changed, and Reggie ended up eating alone. He didn't like that, but what bothered him more was Max's attitude. Max could eat with whomever he liked, but on several occasions he'd come back from his break late, very late. It wasn't right. Max had no respect for his job.

"Reggie, see you in a while," Max called as he slipped an arm around Anabelle.

"You'll be back by one, won't you?"

"Sure," Max promised. Reggie wished he could believe him. Max meant well, but when he got carried away with something he often forgot about everyone else. Reggie wondered about Anabelle, too. He really didn't know her—they nodded and smiled when they ran into each other—but his gut feeling was she was trouble. A different kind of trouble than Hunter, but maybe just as serious. She was beautiful and sweet, sure, but something about her big house, fancy clothes, and family made Reggie assume she was really spoiled. She had Max wrapped around her little finger. Max, of course, thought he had some kind of power over her because he'd taken her away from Hunter, but in Reggie's opinion it was really Anabelle who controlled Max.

"Hey, Harrison," Philip called in a querulous voice. Reggie walked over to his tower, looking up. "Where are the lovebirds heading now?"

"Lunch, I guess."

"He better be back on time."

"He will."

"You think it's fair? He's out that extra time with his chick while we sit here roasting?"

"Don't worry about it," Reggie said quietly. What was bugging Philip?

"I worry, Harrison. He's taking advantage."

"It's not a big deal," Reggie said. He couldn't believe the hypocrisy. Philip, who had hated being a waiter as much as anyone, couldn't wait to come to the beach. He'd practically kissed Max's feet in gratitude. And now he was complaining.

"You know what Max's problem is? He thinks he's special. Head lifeguard and all. He's sure he's better than you and me."

"That's a bunch of bull," said Reggie.

"He thinks he's lord of the beach."

Reggie turned away. Trying to convince Philip was impossible.

"Quit taking his side, Harrison. You don't owe him anything. What's he done for you?" Philip shouted at him.

"I'm not defending him. What's bothering you anyway?" Reggie finally asked.

"How can that Anabelle think Max is such a hotshot? It's not like he's rich or famous or brilliant."

Philip slipped into a T-shirt and hurried down his tower, still annoyed. He gave Reggie a look, as if he were hopelessly out of it, and started toward the road.

"What are you doing?" Reggie said. "You aren't off till one."

"I'm going to the pub for a beer. Want to join me?"

"Hey, be serious."

Philip laughed sarcastically, waving good-bye over one shoulder. "If Max can cut out," he yelled back, "so can I."

CHAPTER 14

Max took Anabelle's hand and led her through the thicket of pines until they reached a clearing. The blanket rippled softly as it went down, then Anabelle emptied the picnic basket. China plates. Cloth napkins. Utensils with carved wooden handles. The sun exploded off the lake, turning it into a glassy field of blinking lights. Max spotted his empty tower, remembering he had to be back at one.

"Not a bad idea," Max complimented Anabelle. They'd had lunch together often, but this was their first picnic provided by Anabelle. "What's this?" He picked up a small jar and made a face.

"Pâté de foie gras. Goose liver, silly."

"And this?" It looked to Max like dried paste.

"One of my favorites. It's called Leek Lorraine. A combination of cheese, peppers, leeks, dry mustard—"

"Delicious," said Max, as he spread some on a cracker and took a bite. It tasted okay, something the Sherborne might serve, but he wasn't wild about it. "You make this?"

"Mom and me. We like to cook. Do you?"

"Do I what?"

"Cook at home much?"

He shrugged. "Only when I have to. I eat out a lot. There's a great burger place near the high school."

Anabelle was laughing, her eyes squinting shut. She put a hand to her mouth to hold in the food.

"What's so hysterical?" Max asked.

"I don't know. Just you."

She was still laughing as Max made her look at him as he told the truth. "Being a lifeguard is just a front. I'm really on a CIA mission to track down a Russian midget named Smirnoff, and after tonight, when I've disposed of my target, I'm going to disappear. Anabelle, forget you've ever seen me, and never divulge what I've told you."

"Don't disappear," she said, half seriously.

"I must."

"I'd be upset."

Max tossed his head back, smiling pensively. "Sometimes I think you wouldn't care, Anabelle."

"Why?" She was surprised.

"My family doesn't have tons of money."

"I know. Who cares?"

"I don't dress too well."

"I'll buy you some clothes," she promised.

"I don't go to a prep school."

"That's why I like you."

"And I'm not totally honest."

Anabelle cocked her head. "What do you mean?"

"I have a confession." He made himself look contrite. "I've been up to this same spot before."

"With another girl?" she said, a little hurt.

"No, by myself. Late at night."

"Doing what?"

"Watching you."

Her brows knitted together. "I don't get it."

"You and Hunter. The most notorious skinny-dippers this side of Philadelphia."

Her face suddenly flushed. "You were spying! How could you, Max? That's not fair—"

She wanted to be angry, but Max was grinning so much she gave up, dropping her head on his shoulder. "You dirty rat," she said.

"Sorry. I had to tell you sooner or later. You were beautiful, you know. You *are* beautiful."

They kissed, a long, deep embrace that took Max by surprise. He pulled her closer to him. His whole body was on fire. But the kiss didn't seem to mean as much to Anabelle because she suddenly pulled back. She gazed out at the lake. Its colors changed as quickly as a chameleon's.

"I used to come up here when I was younger," she said thoughtfully.

"A lot?" Max asked.

"Whenever I got mad at my parents. This was my hideaway."

"What did you do?"

"I just sat and watched the lake. Dreaming. I always came alone. The lake's so beautiful, don't you think?"

Max nodded. "You're lucky you live in Barnswell. There are worse places to grow up," he said sincerely.

"I suppose. But when I was younger, when I was upset, I wanted to be somewhere else."

"Europe?" he guessed.

"Anywhere. I just wanted to escape. Actually," and she suddenly giggled, "I wanted my boyfriend, Billy Sloan, to take me away. I wanted him to spend oodles of money on me, buy me nice clothes, and a car, even a house. Really," she said, amazed at herself, "I think I was only nine or ten."

"Sweet dreams," Max said.

"Did you ever have fantasies like that?"

"Nothing terribly imaginative. I just wanted to be a football player."

"That sounds too dangerous," she worried. "I don't want you ever to get hurt."

They ate mostly in silence, looking out to the lake, throwing down occasional stones. Max checked his watch. "I've got to get back," he said, and began filling up the basket.

"Not yet."

"I have to."

"Not if you don't want to." She put her finger to his lips.

It was wrong, Max thought, he had to get back. But as they stretched out on the blanket, the noise from the beach seemed far away. Max played silently with Anabelle's hair as her head dropped into the crook of his shoulder. They were in a cocoon, warm and safe, shielded from everything. Each kiss was as compelling as a dream.

"I may love you," Anabelle whispered.

Max cradled her head gently. She was too precious to let go, he thought, ever. In a way he was still surprised. How could things have turned out so perfectly? The summer had begun as a disaster. Now it was the sweetest time of his life, and he wanted it to go on forever.

CHAPTER 15

"What do you want to talk about, young man?"

Fitzroy seemed in an agreeable mood as he took a chair on the hotel veranda, the striped awning billowing overhead, and lifted his legs onto a cushioned ottoman. In Bermuda shorts and a Hawaiian-style shirt, his legs looked white as cheese, and blue veins crisscrossed his calves like intersecting highways. Hunter took the chair next to him, feeling frustrated but determined. The sun had started to dip behind the serrated tips of the mountains, lighting up the sky in streaks of red.

"It's quite simple, Mr. Fitzroy. I'd like my job back."

The manager nodded in understanding, as if he'd expected the overture.

"The strike was an unfortunate idea." Hunter forced the words out, hating every second of the confession.

"And the others? What do they think?"

Hunter hadn't seen Skip or Toby in a week. Since the strike had fizzled, they'd cooled to him. He was sure they were thinking he was a loser. "I think they'd be ready to start tomorrow."

"Indeed. Doing what the hotel tells you this time, I hope."

"We're sorry for what we did," Hunter said. He tried to look contrite, but inside he was still full of rage.

Fitzroy coughed uncontrollably into a fist, his face coloring before he got his breath back. "I understand your position, young man. And I appreciate the apology. Unfortunately," he added, lifting his drink to his lips, "I can't give you your jobs back."

"What?" Hunter said slowly.

"Not this summer."

Fitzroy seemed genuinely sorry, but Hunter wasn't in an understanding mood. He wanted to strangle somebody. "We're the regular lifeguards! It's our right to work! We'll accept the hotel's terms. A full seven-day week . . .no increase in pay . . ."

"It's too late. I have a contract with the new group of boys."

"Listen," Hunter snapped, but the words were choked inside. Furious, he levered himself out of his chair. What did Fitzroy want, for him to get down on his knees and beg? He wasn't about to, not for anything. "There's something you should know," Hunter said bitterly. "About your favorite lifeguard. Max Riley. He's not doing such a terrific job."

"That sounds like sour grapes," Fitzroy said, looking at Hunter with pity.

"He skips out for long lunches. One time he was gone all afternoon. But don't take my word for it. . . ."

Hunter turned and left. He couldn't stand facing that creaking fossil another second. Fitzroy only heard what he wanted to hear, which ticked off Hunter all the more. It was true about Max. Hunter had been spying on Anabelle, watching her continually, and she was almost always with the ape man. Hunter had even seen them in the shopping mall where Anabelle had paid for a shirt Max had tried on. Hunter couldn't believe it. What kind of guy was Max anyway?

Hunter drifted downtown toward the video arcade. Kids passing him waved, but he ignored everybody. They were laughing at him, he knew. Just like Fitzroy. He felt it was all a conspiracy—Anabelle, the hotel lackeys, Max. Hunter had never experienced anything like it. To have the rug pulled out from under him. . . . He still felt confused and disoriented. Now that the humiliating confession with Fitzroy had failed, he had to think of something else, and quick. Max was the root of the problem. Maybe he should start with Max. Start and finish. All he had to do, Hunter knew, was be more clever than his enemy.

Hunter stopped outside the arcade, peering in moodily. He couldn't believe that the little wimp from the pub was plugging quarters into a machine. Reggie the Liar. Max's loyal friend. Goofing off after a day at the beach. What a nice surprise, Hunter thought, watching Reggie lose his money.

"Hey you," Hunter called, as Reggie headed outside.

Reggie turned, looked surprised, and kept walking. Hunter caught up with him in the alley behind the ice cream parlor.

"I'm talking to you," said Hunter, pushing a hand out to catch Reggie's elbow. "Translated, that means stop and listen."

Reggie kept his head down. "I'm busy."

"Sure," laughed Hunter. "I want you to give your big shot friend a message."

"Which friend?" Reggie looked up.

"His name starts with an 'M,' pal."

"If you mean Max, you can talk to him yourself. He'll be around any second." Reggie tried to pull away but Hunter pinned him against the wall.

"Oh, I get it," Hunter said. "You two are going to meet, is that it?"

Reggie felt so nervous he could scarcely breathe. "That's right. Six-fifteen. By the ice cream parlor."

"Spare me the tricks, Reggie. We all know where Max is. He's out with Anabelle."

Reggie's cheeks turned puffy and red.

"Let me give you the message anyway," said Hunter calmly. "You see up there?" He pointed. When Reggie glanced up, Hunter pushed a fist cleanly into his gut. Reggie's head flew back, striking the wall, and his body sagged. His mouth jerked open like a fish when the hook is pulled out.

"Leave me alone," Reggie managed to whisper.

"That's the first message," Hunter announced. "Here's the second—"

He dragged Reggie up by his collar and delivered another blow. There wasn't much muscle tissue to protect him. Pathetic, Hunter thought. Big lifeguard. A trickle of blood seeped from Reggie's mouth.

"One more message," Hunter said.

Reggie dropped a hand to protect himself, but Hunter's aim was high, almost at the chest. Reggie's face twisted in pain. He moaned like someone trapped in a nightmare.

"Speak to me, Reggie the Liar," Hunter taunted.

The face stayed blank. Tears fell in silence.

"I'm not finished with you, Reggie." Hunter pulled back his arm, aiming for the jaw, when a fist suddenly attacked him in his kidney. The sting was momentarily paralyzing, and when Hunter staggered up, he watched a second fist coming toward his nose. Duck, he thought, closing his eyes, but the blow knocked him down. Something was squeezing his skull, threatening to crush him. He looked up from the asphalt, bewildered. His face was bloody.

"You," Hunter said, trembling with anger, when Max's hulking figure came into focus.

"How's it feel?" asked Max. When there was no answer, he jabbed a foot into Hunter's body. Hunter howled and bit down on his lip. "Next time you pick on Reggie or anyone else—"

"Don't tell me!" Hunter wheezed, waiting for his breath to come back. "You're causing the problems. Why don't you get the hell out of Barnswell! You don't belong here . . . never will . . ."

Max lifted Reggie to his feet. "Listen to this guy, Reggie. Hunter thinks he can give orders. Like he's in charge here. Personally, I think he's gone soft in the head."

"I'm warning you," Hunter wheezed.

Max made a motion to strike him again. Hunter covered his head. "My, what courage," quipped Max. He helped Reggie out of the alley and left the mess on the ground.

"Maybe you should see a doctor," Max said when he and Reggie were alone. He peeked under Reggie's shirt. "Your ribs look pretty bruised."

Reggie straightened up slowly, testing his body for soreness. "I think I'm just winded."

"He could have hurt you."

"He tried. Like I always said he would."

"Yeah, yeah, I know—he's crazy." They walked along the sidewalk with Reggie's arm draped over Max's shoulder. "But he knows to lay off now. At least he better."

"I guess I should thank you for coming to my rescue," said Reggie quietly.

"For what? Saving you? Forget it. I told you we were friends." Max sat Reggie on a bench in front of a drug store. "Let me get some ice. It'll keep down the swelling."

"I'll be okay," Reggie insisted.

"At least take a couple days off from work."

"No," he protested. "Everything's all right."

Max was suddenly smiling. "You know, you're just as stubborn as I am. Maybe we should have been in the same family—I always wanted a brother."

CHAPTER 16

"Saturday night we're having our first annual Lifeguards-For-A-Cleaner-Beach party," Max announced as the others ringed him in a loose circle in front of his tower. "We drink a lot of beer, and then we clean up our cans . . ."

Reggie laughed along with Tiny, but Philip and Kenny were quiet, as if too tired from their long day to appreciate Max's humor. The lake traffic was starting to thin out since it was already after five, but Reggie kept a concerned eye on the few kids near the outer string of buoys.

"Try again," Philip said to Max. With his arms crossed over his chest, Philip looked cocky, almost belligerent. "I'll probably be busy this Saturday."

"What about Friday?" Max asked.

"Maybe. Maybe not."

Max set his mouth in deliberation. "You wouldn't be trying to be difficult, Philip."

"Not as difficult as you are. At least I'm on the job when I'm supposed to be, oh fearless leader."

"Come on," Tiny interrupted. "Let's talk about the party. How many girls are coming? I say Friday's fine."

Max's gaze swung to the others. Reggie nodded, and Kenny did too. Philip remained pouty.

"What about Washington?" Philip asked. "He's still part of the cabin, isn't he? Or maybe you've forgotten about him."

"No one's leaving Washington out," Max said. "If you want, we'll talk about the party at the cabin tonight."

"You mean if you're there," Philip said dryly.

"What's your problem?" Tiny turned on Philip. "You're becoming a royal pain in the butt. You had a great time at our first party, and all of a sudden you're above it all."

"The only guy above it all is Max. It's pretty obvious, isn't it? Kenny feels the same way as I do."

"No," Kenny said quickly. He looked flustered when everybody stared. "I mean, not really."

"You told me," Philip pressured him.

"What I said was that sometimes Max forces his ideas on us." Kenny grew fidgety and avoided looking at Max. Since the first group activities, Kenny had grown moody and depressed. Reggie knew why. Kenny was a glutton for guilt. Every night Reggie noticed that he wrote a letter to his girlfriend. When Kenny once left a letter uncovered Reggie saw it was full of apologies and disenchantment with his summer. Whether Kenny admitted getting drunk and partying with another girl, Reggie doubted, but he was obviously anxious about Max's determination for the cabin to party and have fun.

"Quit making trouble," Tiny warned Philip.

"Mind your own business," he snapped back.

The silence became awkward as everyone stared out at the lake. Two young boys began fighting by the boat docks, and Tiny hustled over to break them apart. Philip and Kenny slowly wandered back to their towers.

"Philip's just jealous," Reggie said to Max when they were alone.

"Yeah," he said indifferently.

"It's not the end of the world. So what if he doesn't come to the party?" Reggie felt a little sorry for Max.

"Who cares about the party anyway," Max said suddenly. He looked peeved. "I'm getting tired of putting up with the lack of appreciation around here. Philip's just part of it. Although I figured he'd turn against me. He's really one of them, belongs here in Barnswell. It's a bunch of crap what I have to take. The hotel rules, the guests. Being at everyone's beck and call. Always busting my butt to please."

"It's been easier being a lifeguard than a waiter."

Max smiled at Reggie's thick-headedness. "True, but we're still their servants."

"What?"

"Look around you, Reggie. What do you see?" asked Max.

Reggie didn't know what Max wanted. He glanced out at the lake, back to the hotel, and up the shore road to the town. "The same things that I see every day."

"You're looking, but you're not seeing. Do you notice all those Mercedes and Porsches, the big houses, the clothes in the stores, the jewelry people wear—"

"What about them?" Reggie interrupted.

"Don't you ever dream about owning things like those?"

Reggie shook his head. He never really had.

"When I'm with Anabelle," Max admitted, "sometimes I can't think of anything else. Her world is nothing but luxury."

"So?" said Reggie. "Who cares about Anabelle's world? What's important is Anabelle."

"You can't exactly ignore her surroundings, Reggie. The house, the cars, the money—they're part of her life. They're part of her."

"What are you saying? If Anabelle were from a poor family, you wouldn't be just as happy with her?"

"Of course I'd love her," Max said quickly, embarrassed by Reggie's question. "But you're missing the point."

"What's the point?"

"Doesn't it bother you being poor? Don't you ever ask yourself why they have everything and we have nothing?"

Reggie had to laugh. "You mean the people in Barnswell? They're established. That's why they have money. We're only summer help."

"That's for sure," Max said. "This is my last summer being a slave. When I get out of school I'm splitting for California. I'm going to sell real estate and make more money than these clowns ever dreamed about."

"Great," Reggie offered, "if that's what you want."

Max shot him a look of disbelief. Reggie realized that Max didn't understand why somebody wouldn't want all the money he could put his hands on—didn't understand what could be more important. To Reggie money wasn't his ultimate goal, nor did he consider himself low man on the totem pole this summer. The Sherborne was just a job. The crucial thing was that he wouldn't let himself be a lifeguard, or a waiter for the rest of his life.

"You really amaze me, Reggie. Pure as the driven snow. Don't you ever dream? What are you going to do with your life—hole up in a monastery?"

Reggie was quiet, pushing his foot through the sand. "I'll probably go to college. If I'm smart enough, maybe I'll try law school. Anyway, that's what my dad wanted."

"What do you mean, *wanted*? He giving you a hard time now?"

Reggie molded the sand into a small mountain. The words came out slowly. "My dad was killed in a car accident."

Max looked at him, surprised.

"Last Christmas," Reggie said.

"That must have been tough. I'm really sorry. You never told us."

"Yeah."

"Are you okay now?"

"Fine," Reggie said quickly, then in the silence returned to his tower. For a moment Max had looked at him knowingly, as if Reggie's admission about his father's death had explained something. Reggie felt a rare moment of relief. He had actually talked to somebody about the accident. Someone besides his mother and his shrink. And Max seemed to care.

"Hey, Reggie," Max shouted over the roar of the outboards a few minutes later. He was putting on his jeans. "Do me a favor—keep an eye on the beach. I have to leave a little early. I'm meeting Anabelle . . ."

Reggie waved that it was okay, but he wondered how Max managed not to care that Philip was hot and bothered, and that the others were getting upset, too. Why did Max push his luck? Couldn't Anabelle wait half an hour until they were off duty? Max was always rushing things. The jump from waiter to lifeguard had been overnight. His romance with Anabelle was a whirlwind. His envy about everyone else being loaded while he was poor, and his desire to make his bundle soon—what was the big hurry?

Reggie watched as Max, halfway to the shore road, suddenly pivoted and marched back toward the towers. Reggie was puzzled until he spied Fitzroy standing by the road like a stone sentry. A hand shielded his eyes from the glare.

"Can you believe that?" Max said when he reached Reggie. "My good Irish buddy, Fitzroy, is checking up on us."

"It had to happen sooner or later. Word probably got back to him about guards cutting out early."

"From whom?"

Reggie shrugged. "Hotel guests. Hunter. Maybe even Philip."

"Terrific." Max picked up a handful of sand and stared at it moodily. Then he glanced anxiously to town.

"Forget it," said Reggie. "You can't go."

"I have to. I have something for Anabelle." Max reached into his jeans for two neatly folded pieces of paper. "She's meeting me at Lord Michael's in five minutes. At six she has to leave with her parents for a dinner party."

"What's that?" Reggie stared at the paper.

Max hesitated. "I can't tell you."

Reggie looked for a trace of a smile, but Max was serious. "Why's it so important?"

"If I told anybody, it would be you. But this is personal, okay?" Max twisted around to check on Fitzroy. His baggy pants blew like tent flaps in the wind. "I'm going anyway," he decided.

"Don't be dumb," Reggie said. "You'll jeopardize everyone's job." Reggie didn't care where he spent the rest of the summer, but seeing Max back in the kitchen, or out of work, bothered him. It wasn't fair, after he'd been so clever and persistent, for all of them. Blinded by Anabelle, Max obviously couldn't see the danger.

"Give me the notes," said Reggie after a moment. He fought back his doubts, "I'll go for you."

"You don't have to—"

"Fitzroy won't do anything to me. The complaints have all been about you, I'm sure. If I'm stopped, I'll say I'm going to see the nurse."

Max's forehead furrowed in deliberation. "You sure you want to do this?"

"You think I'm afraid of going to Lord Michael's?" said Reggie, as he put on his jeans.

"I guess not. You wouldn't have volunteered. Thanks . . . I mean it."

Reggie did feel uneasy as he trotted over the beach toward town, but Fitzroy scarcely glanced at him. Reggie had imagined too much, as usual. He was tired of blowing things out of proportion and angry at himself for inventing difficulties that intimidated him. As he walked into Lord Michael's there was no sign of Hunter. Anabelle was at a corner table, her face reflected in a window.

"Hi," said Reggie, stuffing his hands awkwardly in his front pockets. Anabelle looked at him, puzzled. "Max sent me," he explained.

"Is something wrong?" she asked quickly.

"Max is fine. He just couldn't get away," Reggie said. "Fitzroy was keeping an eye on the beach this afternoon."

Anabelle was disappointed, Reggie could tell. He wondered if he should stick around. Part of him wanted to hand over the notes and get out. But Anabelle was signaling to the waitress. "Would you like something?" she asked Reggie.

He ordered a beer and sat down self-consciously. He still felt distrustful of Anabelle, and coupled with his shyness, he had nothing to say.

"Max really likes you," Anabelle said suddenly. "He considers you a close friend." She put her lips to her coffee cup and blew away the steam. "He's told me more than once."

Reggie was surprised by the compliment, but flattered. "I'm the only one who puts up with him," he joked.

She smiled. "Where are you from?"

"Troy," he answered. He wished he had more to say.

"Do you like Barnswell?"

"It's okay."

"But not great?" she asked.

"I'm not crazy about it," he admitted.

Anabelle smiled knowingly, as if she wasn't totally wild

about the town either. Reggie couldn't help thinking that, while Anabelle was nice, she was also a little phony. Barnswell meant a lot to her. It had to. She was the prettiest girl in town. Everyone knew and respected her family. She was on a pedestal all her own.

"What do you think of Max?" she asked suddenly.

"I like him."

"Do you know him well?"

"I'm starting to."

"Well," and she hesitated, playing with the coffee mug, "what do you think of us as a couple?"

Now Reggie knew why Anabelle had asked him to sit down. He wanted to tell her that he thought their relationship was too sudden, that it was hard to believe it would last, but he only said, "I think you two are great together." His face reddened from the lie.

"I'm not embarrassing you, am I?" she said thoughtfully.

"No." He tried to look relaxed.

"I'm really fond of Max, but some people think that's crazy. I wondered about your opinion."

"Sure, anytime," he said casually. He could just imagine Anabelle coming to him whenever something was up with Max. The waitress brought the beer and Reggie gulped at it.

"What does Max say about me?" Anabelle asked.

"What?"

"Does he talk about me to you? You're his friend, after all."

"You mean a lot to him." Reggie felt better. That was easy.

"How much is a lot?" Anabelle looked him in the eye.

"You know Max. He's impulsive. He sometimes gets carried away. You're on his mind all the time."

"But you don't think our relationship will last," she interpreted. "He's impulsive, he'll change—"

"No, no," Reggie interrupted "He's really crazy about you. Of course it will last."

Anabelle went back to her coffee. She seemed relieved. Reggie felt foolish. "Here," he said, fumbling for the notes in his pocket. "These are from Max."

Anabelle's eyes raced down the first sheet. She seemed amused. "Max never gives up, does he?"

"What do you mean?"

"He's been asking me to introduce him to my father for ages. I didn't think it was a good idea. Now Max has given me a letter, and one for my father. He wants to discuss a business deal. He wants me to talk to my dad about this tonight."

Reggie was surprised. He'd figured the notes would be a poem or a love letter, something like Kenny might write. But it was about business. Crazy. Anabelle's father owned a lot of property and businesses in town, Max had confided to Reggie. Maybe, since he loved money so much, Max smelled an opportunity. No one ever accused him of lacking nerve.

Reggie finished his beer, ready to leave, but Anabelle was already up. "I've got to run," she said. "It was nice talking to you, Reggie. I hope we can meet again."

"Sure."

"You know what I like about you?" she said, as an afterthought. He sat back, waiting. "You're honest. You have an honest face."

Reggie turned his eyes away as Anabelle left. He rose wearily and wandered out of the pub. No one was around to bother him.

Anabelle wasn't so bad, he conceded as he headed back to the hotel. She had a lot of poise and determination, and she was full of life. On some levels, she and Max really were compatible. As Reggie skirted the beach he saw that Fitzroy had disappeared along with most of the guests. A sleek blue outboard from the hotel zigzagged toward the middle of the lake, making splashy turns, hamming it up for any spectators. The driver was tall and broad shouldered, and fitted with a neon orange life jacket. Reggie looked again. It was Max.

Max was in his heaven as he turned the boat at will. The speed, the power, the freedom. Reggie wished he had a camera. The picture would have been up to Max's expectations. It would have been worth a million.

CHAPTER 17

The headlights drifted over the winding road, making a path in the darkness. Max steered in a daze. He was vaguely aware that they were nearing Barnswell, that it was late, and that the Mercedes was almost on empty. Nothing mattered. Anabelle's head nestled on his shoulder and her left hand lightly touched his leg. They had been driving in silence since leaving the mountain cottage. It all still seemed like a dream to Max. Anabelle had arrived at the beach that afternoon and invited Max to take a ride in her father's car. He'd cut out early, and they'd ended up at her family's cottage half an hour away. They had walked in the woods, picked berries, and with a bottle of wine, taken a rowboat out on a nearby lake.

When Anabelle asked mischievously, "Do you feel bad for leaving the beach early?" Max just laughed.

He felt the glow of his dreams unfolding. Anabelle might deny it, but he felt sure she was growing more dependent on him by the day. He no longer worried that Anabelle still liked Hunter. Her former boyfriend was nothing but a monument to history. Anabelle was Max's now, and nothing would change that.

The car coasted down a final hill when the smell of smoke hit Max. Faint, darkish, slightly unpleasant—like burned coffee. Something was wrong with the car, he worried. Then he saw the flames in the near distance. Anabelle shot up in her seat as if pinched.

"It's on the beach," she said for both of them.

Max looked harder. "Hey—that's my tower!"

A fire truck was parked nearby with hoses stretched out over the sand, entwined like a pair of snakes. The Fourth of July one month late, Max thought, incredulous. In the midst of the flames the scorched beams resembled a mosaic of tiny crosses. Hissing eerily, the fireball reflected on the dark lake. With the first blast from a fire hose the tower groaned and toppled.

Max took Anabelle's hand and hurried down. He spotted Kenny among the ring of spectators. "What happened?" Max demanded.

"I don't know. I was walking along the lake before I went back to the cabin. The fire erupted out of nowhere," Kenny explained.

"You didn't see anyone down here?" Max prodded him. Kenny shook his head, but his face looked distraught. "Hey, what's the matter?" Max asked. He went to lay a hand on Kenny's shoulder but Kenny ducked the gesture and walked away.

"What's wrong with him?" Anabelle asked.

"I don't know. Something's screwy."

"What started the fire?" Anabelle asked.

Max answered darkly, "You mean who."

Anabelle flashed her eyes to the blackened rubble. "Max, do you think it was Hunter?"

"Who else," he said glumly. "This is supposed to be some sort of warning. It's my tower."

"Hunter can be so childish. If he stooped to this—"

"He's going too far."

"You have to understand him, Max. He's always gotten what he wanted. You're the first person to stand in his way."

"So he does this? Reggie was right—Hunter's a maniac."

Max watched, depressed, as the firemen pulled their hoses back to the truck. Tomorrow morning he'd be responsible for cleaning up the mess. And if he knew Fitzroy, somehow the hotel manager would put some of the blame on him. Fitzroy always held someone responsible, and there was no one else to finger.

It might even be worse, Max realized as he led Anabelle to the car. Fitzroy could fire him, just like he had Hunter. Too much trouble. So what? he suddenly thought. There was almost something liberating about getting sacked. Free, he'd have more time with Anabelle. And if he could work something out with her father, he'd have money, too.

"Did you give your father my letter?" Max asked casually as he drove Anabelle home.

"Maybe," she teased.

"Anabelle—"

"I gave it to him last night. I was going to tell you."

"What did he say?"

"Honestly? He thought the letter was pushy and presumptuous."

Max began to worry. "I just asked him for a job. I want to work in one of his stores after school next year. I'll get a lift over from Bradley and be here by three-thirty every day. I'm giving up football for this."

"That would be nice," she said.

"So what was presumptuous?"

"The other part of your letter. You said 'if you were a good worker, you wanted to manage the store.' Daddy already has a manager."

"But I'll do a better job than that guy," Max said quickly.

"No problem at all." He felt a small hole opening in his stomach. Maybe Anabelle's father wasn't going to be so easy to win over.

"Don't be silly. You're only sixteen."

"What's age have to do with anything?" He was suddenly annoyed. "Whose side are you on, anyway?"

She smiled mysteriously. "Yours."

"Doesn't sound like it."

Anabelle slipped an arm through Max's. "After Daddy finished his negative comments, I told him he was wrong, that you'd be a terrific employee, and that he'd be a fool not to hire you. I also told him I'd be surprised if you weren't running more than one store by the time I got back from school next summer."

A smile came slowly to Max's lips. "You're a doll."

"I meant every word. I believe in you," she said, squeezing his hand. "That's why I want you to come to dinner Saturday. You can meet Daddy and talk."

"At your house?" Max was pleasantly surprised.

"I promise, no pâté."

Max remembered the beach party he had tentatively planned. Philip was still being difficult, and Max had grown impatient. Why should he always be doing things for the cabin? Except for Reggie, no one fully appreciated his efforts.

"I'll be there," said Max. "Can I bring something?"

"Nothing." She thought again. "Yes. You can bring Reggie."

"What?"

"I want you to invite Reggie. He's nice. Unless you don't want to . . ."

"No, I'll bring him," Max promised.

"Eight o'clock."

She shivered from the night dampness as Max helped her

out of the car. At the back door she unclasped the key from her neck chain and slipped it into the lock.

"Thanks for coming with me to the cottage and making this a special day," she said, turning to face him. Her hand gently touched his neck. "I've really fallen for you, Max Riley—in case you haven't noticed. Just don't let it go to your head."

"I won't. Scout's honor."

She put her hand on the door. "Good night."

"Can't I come in?" he asked.

"It's late."

"Just for a few minutes—"

"You'd better go," she said, more firmly. "My parents might be up. It wouldn't be the best time to meet my father."

"Okay." He smiled but he was hurt. If Anabelle really loved him, why was she so distant at times? Resigned, he turned to leave.

"Wait a minute, Max . . . don't be upset." Catching up, she wrapped her arms around his neck, pushed up off her toes, and kissed him tenderly on the lips. "Did I surprise you?"

He went to kiss her back but she pulled away.

"I want you to surprise me, too," she whispered.

Max was confused. What kind of game was she playing? "What do you mean?" he asked.

She looked at him, her soft hazel eyes so promising and mysterious, and then she pressed her key into his hand.

CHAPTER 18

The house was on fire, Max thought. Clouds of coarse smoke drifted into the living room like a black fog, coating the air. The smell reminded him of the burning lifeguard tower. He looked around anxiously before he noticed the barbecue grill through the window, the bright orange flames leaping up. Max hurried over to close the patio door.

Turning back, he almost bumped into Mrs. Livingston as she brought over frosted glasses of ginger ale. Reggie took his silently, but Max made a point to praise the hostess and her house effusively. Mrs. Livingston smiled in appreciation. They were dumb comments, not terribly original, but Max figured it was hard to over flatter. Straightening his tie, he settled back on the couch with Reggie.

The house really *was* special, he thought, glancing around. Revolutionary War period antiques. Currier and Ives prints. Oil paintings hanging over fieldstone hearths. One bookcase alone held a dozen shiny black photos of Livingston ancestors from the Civil War. Mrs. Livingston had called the photos daguerreotypes.

"My husband and his brother were born in this house," Mrs. Livingston explained, sitting across from Max. "It's been in their family since 1800."

"Incredible," Max volunteered, but Reggie didn't act impressed at all. For a moment Max wished he hadn't brought him.

"I'm from Barnswell, too," Mrs. Livingston went on. "I think half this town was born here. We hope that Anabelle will stay and raise her family here. That is, after she goes to Smith and graduates, like her mother and grandmother before her. I know it's hard for young people to come back to their roots, and society today is so mobile . . . but we hope . . ."

". . . and pray," a voice chimed in from the kitchen. Mr. Livingston smiled facetiously as he marinated the steaks. Still, Max knew he was serious. Anabelle kept a poker face as she helped in the kitchen.

"I remember you well from the Sherborne," Mrs. Livingston spoke to Max. "You were a terribly conscientious waiter. But now Anabelle says you're working on the beach."

"We're lifeguards," Max said, but Mrs. Livingston had to know. Maybe Hunter had even given her his side of the story, how Max had taken away his job and all.

"There was that terrible fire a couple of nights ago," she said.

"Just one tower," Reggie put in.

"I think it was a prankster, don't you?" asked Mrs. Livingston.

Max said nothing. Prankster, sure. He had spent three hours cleaning up the debris, then faced an annoyed Fitzroy. The manager had stopped short of asking Max to pay for a new tower, but he was determined to punish Max anyway. He would resume his duties without a tower for the rest of the season. He was also to sign in and out with the hotel every day, as were the other guards, to guarantee that everyone kept honest hours. Max thought Fitzroy really believed his guys had caused the fire. Max wanted to quit on the spot, but payday wasn't till Tuesday.

"Are you enjoying your work?" Mrs. Livingston asked.

"Sure," said Reggie. "It's better than being a waiter."

"Well, not totally," Max interjected. "It's a job, but I'd like something more challenging. Something with a future."

"Of course. You have to think of your future. How about you, Reggie?"

Max relaxed a degree. He had Mrs. Livingston figured. The proper hostess. The proper mother and wife who didn't offer controversial opinions, find fault, or make anyone feel uncomfortable. A peacemaker. That was nice, he thought. Max excused himself and walked into the kitchen.

"Can I help anyone?" he said.

"No, thanks. Everything's under control." Anabelle gave Max a wink, as if to tell him they had to be on their best behavior tonight. Mr. Livingston was dicing onions for a barbecue sauce.

"Sure, you can help," he announced in a robust voice. "Put on an apron." He peered over his bifocals like a courtroom judge to scrutinize Max. "I'm going to let you cook the steaks."

"Daddy—"

"What's wrong with that? Max asked to help. There's no law against a guest pitching in, is there?"

"No, sir," Max said as he tied the apron around him. Mr. Livingston shoved the platter of steaks into his hands.

"We all like them medium rare. That's pink, not red, in the center. How do you like yours?"

"The same," Max answered.

"You aren't just trying to be agreeable?" Mr. Livingston inquired. Max denied it. "Good. I don't like 'yes' people."

Max moved outside with the meat. He wondered about Mr. Livingston. He was candid, slightly sarcastic, a quick talker. A bit different from the man who'd tipped Max generously at the restaurant. Or maybe tonight was a test.

"I read your letter over again." Mr. Livingston hovered like a shadow as Max splayed the steaks over the grill. The juice splattered up from the hot coals.

"You've got ambition. I can see that," he offered.

"Yes, sir."

"But Anabelle tells me you don't want to go to college. She finds that notion romantic—for some strange reason."

"I'd rather be out earning money," Max explained.

"I thought that's why one went to college, for a better job."

"Some people do," Max conceded. "For me it would just be marking time. I'm planning to go to California and sell real estate."

"And in the meantime you want to work for me. Build a nest egg for Beverly Hills. Or are you more interested in spending time with my Anabelle?"

"Well, I would be able to see her whenever she gets vacation."

"Would you say, Max, that you're rather attracted to my daughter?"

"Very much." Max ducked his head out of the smoke. His eyes were burning.

"You sound sincere."

"I am, sir."

"You know, I worry about my daughter."

Max nodded. This was becoming an inquisition.

"I wouldn't want her hurt in any way, or for anyone to take advantage—"

"No, sir." He jabbed a fork into the smallest steak and flipped it over.

"That's not ready to be turned," Mr. Livingston pointed out. Max flipped it back. "I like sincerity in people, Max.

Sincerity leads to trust. On the other hand, I don't care for prevaricators. They make me angry."

Max wasn't sure what a prevaricator was. As Mr. Livingston splashed on his barbecue sauce, the smoke billowed up fiercely. Max closed his eyes again. It was going to be a long night.

When dinner was ready Max took the chair next to Anabelle. Her hand sneaked under the table to squeeze his. "Don't worry," she whispered. "Daddy just acts tough. Underneath he's all mush." Max wanted to believe her but something made him skeptical. Mr. Livingston dominated the dinner conversation as if he were running for office. He praised the conservative administration and railed against the liberals. He worried out loud about the economy, protested the taxes he had to pay, and made arguments for higher military expenditures. Max had little to say.

"Who wants some coffee?" Mrs. Livingston asked, when it was time for dessert. Anabelle brought in a chocolate cake, smiling at Max. He knew she'd baked it for him. Still, as he ate, he could hardly taste it since he was thinking about the evening being a bomb. Anabelle, suddenly looking upset herself, motioned to her father. They retreated to the kitchen.

"That was a great meal, Mrs. Livingston," said Max, keeping one eye on the kitchen. "Better than we get at the hotel. Right, Reggie?"

"The best," he answered, but his answer came too slowly.

The kitchen door suddenly slammed closed. Behind it, voices rose and fell in combat. At the table everyone looked away uncomfortably. "They have a very candid relationship," Mrs. Livingston finally said. That was an understatement, Max thought. When silence abruptly dropped over the house it was almost as unsettling as the fighting.

Mr. Livingston appeared first, and Anabelle took her seat right after him. "I'd like to make a toast," he announced, as he playfully raised his coffee mug, "to Max Riley."

The sudden cheerfulness threw Max. Everyone brought his mug up reflexively, but Max was still suspicious. Mr. Livingston smiled benignly. "To Max Riley and Livingston Hardware Stores!"

"Here-here," said Anabelle.

"Thank you," Max said, daring to hope.

"Starting September, you'll work directly under my manager. I'll start you above minimum. If you're conscientious and do a crackerjack job, I'll push it higher. Who knows, maybe you'll have a future in Barnswell."

"That's very gracious, Mr. Livingston. I was just wondering—" The eyes peered over the glasses again, trying to anticipate. Max knew what he was about to ask was gutsy, but he was used to taking chances. That was the only way to succeed. "I was wondering if it were possible to start even before September. Like next Wednesday, sir." Right after he got his hotel paycheck.

"Why so quickly?"

"Frankly, sir, lifeguarding has become rather boring. And this way, starting in your store early, I could learn the ropes."

"An eager beaver. Very commendable. But how do I know you won't be sneaking off with Anabelle?"

"You have my word."

"Promises," he reflected good naturedly. "If I had a dollar for all the promises I've been made, I could buy this state. Okay, Max. Just for you, I'll start you on Wednesday."

Mr. Livingston's large hand arched slowly over the table like a moving bridge. It grabbed Max's and pumped it warmly. Max felt a swell of relief. He was more than thankful, he was overjoyed. The evening had been tense and difficult, but things had worked out. Anabelle had gone to bat for him. He loved her.

In four more days his future would begin. Sure, four or five bucks an hour was a measly wage, but unlike working at the Sherborne, Max would have something going. If he impressed everyone he could end up running the store. Mr. Livingston practically owned the town. Who could say, one day they might even become partners. California would have to wait. Max had money to make in Barnswell.

At the door Max and Reggie thanked Mrs. Livingston for the evening, then Max turned to shake Mr. Livingston's hand again, sealing their agreement. He wanted to kiss Anabelle good night, but somehow, with her parents looking on, it was pushing things, even for him.

"What do you mean, the beach has become boring?" Reggie said as soon as they were out of earshot. He shook his head, dismayed. "You can't quit."

"Why not?" Max said confidently.

"You gave me a big speech why I had to take Washington's place, or else I'd be letting down the whole cabin. We'll all lose our jobs, you said. But now, when you want out—"

"You aren't blaming me, are you? Wouldn't you do the same thing in my position?"

Reggie looked up at the bright light of the stars, thinking. "I don't know."

"Of course you would. Hey, this is my future, Reggie. And don't worry about the beach. I'll get a replacement."

"Yeah."

"I will! Everything's going to be peachy."

"You're really cocky, you know that?"

"I've got it made, Reggie. I'm working for the fat cat of Barnswell." For a moment Max wondered if maybe he was being too ambitious. Was he stepping on anyone's toes, making any new enemies besides Hunter and his pals? Max hoped not. He didn't want to offend. He just wanted his own place under the sun.

"So?" said Reggie. "Am I supposed to think you'll bust your butt for Mr. Livingston like you did for the hotel?"

"That's hitting below the belt. The Sherborne's irrelevant." Max meant it. Maybe he had squirreled around too much this summer, but that was because it didn't count. The future would be different. "Hey, what was with you tonight anyway?" Max asked suddenly. "The Livingstons live like kings and you acted like the house was a tenement."

"I don't know. The house was nice, so were Anabelle and her mother. It was Mr. Livingston. He was stuffy. He hardly said boo to me."

"He's a nice guy. You'll see. And you didn't say much yourself."

But Max wasn't about to argue. Reggie didn't understand. He was too distrustful of everyone, especially those with money. Max stuffed his hands in his pockets and whistled softly. He couldn't have been happier. In the distance, the town lights shone unevenly into the blackness of the mountains, a field of jewels on a cloth of velvet.

CHAPTER 19

Reggie hurried along the street with his head down. As black clouds rumbled overhead he pulled his jacket collar around him. Like an unwelcome stranger, a cold rain had arrived before dawn, a drizzle that broke into a downpour, then slackened, and now it threatened to hammer down in sheets. Hotel guests had stood on the veranda after breakfast, hoping the skies would clear. One by one they drifted back to their rooms or the lounges. Those who went on to church didn't mind, but Reggie knew most guests were peeved.

Max had been delighted as the lake bubbled and foamed like some sizzling crater. With the beach closed, he hurried over to Anabelle's. Tiny had wandered down to the video arcade, Philip went after a redhead at another hotel, and Kenny had slipped away somewhere, his mood as dark as the weather. The peace of an empty cabin had been a luxury to Reggie. He had read for a couple of hours and left for the movie theater.

Barnswell looked almost ghostly in its gray haze, Reggie thought. The streets were virtually deserted. The pinging of rain on rooftops sounded like a sorcerer's dance. Reggie ducked into a drugstore next to the theater and began thumbing through the latest issue of *Time*. Deliberately, he hadn't picked up a paper or news magazine all summer. They depressed him too much. He could see now that the world was still going bananas.

"Hey, Reg, sorry I'm late, man."

Washington walked into the drugstore without an umbrella, drenched. "What time's the movie start?"

"About fifteen minutes ago, but that's okay."

Washington's moon face furrowed in disappointment. "Carlton wouldn't let me off any sooner."

"So we'll see it in the middle."

"Miss the beginning of a thriller? I wanna be scared, man. We'll make the next show."

They wandered through a few shops and ended up at Lord Michael's. The pub was packed twenty deep with kids who normally would have been on the beach. The smell of pizza made Reggie slightly nauseous. "Welcome to sardine city," Washington said, as they sidled into a booth. They both ordered sodas.

"So how's it in the dining room?" Reggie asked. He hadn't seen Washington much lately, just coming and going, like two ships passing in the night.

"The pits of the universe. But it's probably better than being on the beach."

Reggie didn't get it. "The beach is great."

"All you lifeguards do is fight. You're a bunch of old ladies every night. Party . . . no party. Max never in his tower. Now Philip's not showing up . . ."

"We'll survive."

Reggie glanced up when the sodas came. His eye wandered past the waitress to the bar. He looked again. Hunter was gazing at his beer as if it were a crystal ball, and on the next stool, nodding and talking, sat Kenny Homer.

"What's going on?" Reggie asked, nudging Washington.

Washington turned to look. "Yeah, I know," he said.

"You know? You know what?"

"I saw 'em together a couple days ago."

"Why would Kenny be with Hunter?" Reggie asked.

"Who cares? Kenny never talks to me. He doesn't talk to anybody. What difference does it all make?"

"I guess it's nothing," said Reggie, finally.

At the theater they found center-row seats and made themselves comfortable, but Reggie's thoughts kept jumping to Hunter and Kenny. What were they talking about, and if they'd met twice, were the meetings just coincidence? Max had told Reggie he'd seen Kenny by the burning lifeguard tower. Everyone was convinced Hunter had started the blaze, but maybe he put Kenny up to it. Reggie caught himself. He had no evidence. And the concept sounded preposterous. There he was, seeing the dark side of things again.

The rain had stopped by the time the movie got out. The day was still raw and damp, card-playing weather, Reggie thought, as Washington hurried back to his kitchen duties. At the hotel Reggie looked vainly for Max, then headed up the winding streets to Anabelle's. He decided to ring the bell. When the door opened with a flourish, Max was smiling like a Cheshire cat.

"Don't just stand there, come on in," Max said. The smug grin refused to die. Reggie entered reluctantly, feeling like a trespasser, just as he had last night. Except for the blaze roaring in the den fireplace, the house was silent.

"Where is everybody?" Reggie asked.

"At a church social. Mr. and Mrs. Livingston are always gone on Sundays. But Anabelle promised to be back by three."

"So what are you doing here? Who started the fireplace going?"

Instead of answering, Max flopped into an oversized leather chair and propped his legs on an ottoman. "Tough life, huh, Reggie?"

Reggie marveled at Max's boldness. What was next? Max would probably ask for his own room. "The Livingstons don't know you're here?"

"So?"

"So this isn't exactly your house. And you're not an old family friend."

"There you go again, Reggie. Worrying about what's proper."

"I don't worry, but the Livingstons do."

Max smiled patiently, as if he had to humor Reggie. "I came over this morning and had breakfast with Anabelle. Okay? Then everybody left for church. I left too. But I didn't have anywhere to go. And it was miserable outside. So," he added blithely, "I came back." He held up Anabelle's house key with a wink.

"Never mind," Reggie said after a moment. He turned to the door. "See you later."

"Where are you going? Come on back. I'll get a couple beers from the fridge. Mr. Livingston's not going to walk in. Do you think I'd be sticking around if he was?"

It was still wrong to be in the house, Reggie knew. Maybe Max wasn't dumb enough to be caught, but he was so arrogant. He thought he was invincible. Max actually was a lot like Hunter. The thought was painful to Reggie. So was the realization that Max was probably setting himself up for a fall.

Since last night's bizarre dinner with the Livingstons, Reggie had done a lot of thinking. He liked Max and Anabelle—they were the only people who reacted to his feelings—and he wished them well. But something just didn't *feel* right. Reggie realized that Max sensed the sleepiness of Barnswell and was determined to take it by storm, but what Max didn't quite understand, just as he didn't realize his own vulnerability, was that under the sleepy surface there were roots and rules. They were deep, private, and strong. Maybe Max saw them, but he didn't believe they were anything his ambition couldn't overcome. Reggie thought otherwise.

"Why don't we go for a walk," he suggested to Max.

"Why?" he said lazily. "It's more comfortable here."

"I'd like to talk to you."

"So talk." Max stretched up his stockinged feet to the fire.

"You're not going to like what I have to tell you."

"You're getting me nervous," Max joked. "What happened—is the lake flooding?"

Reggie sat cross-legged on a Persian rug and looked at his friend. "First of all, I'm worried that it's not going to work out for you and Anabelle."

Max gave a smirk. "Good old Reggie, always up."

"I wanted to tell you, that's all."

"What's going to happen?" Max asked coolly.

"I think you'll probably get hurt." Max only looked amused, but to Reggie the anticipation of pain, anyone's pain, made him uneasy. To be surprised, to feel the earth crumble under your feet, then to be left alone . . . What Reggie had gone through with his father had taught him something. Max may have acted tough and invincible, but underneath Reggie saw an ordinary nice guy who was sensitive. "Sooner or later," Reggie said, "Anabelle's going to drop you."

"You've always had something against Anabelle."

"You're wrong. I like her."

"So what's the problem?" Max said impatiently.

Reggie tried to explain. "Have you really looked around this house? It's full of history. Did you hear what Mrs. Livingston said about the people in Barnswell being born here, and she wants Anabelle to stay, too?"

"What about the house? I like it," Max said stubbornly.

Reggie grimaced. "You told me about looking but not seeing. You're the one who's not seeing now. Theirs is a special world, Max. And you don't belong in it."

"So they're rich, and I'm not. I know about our differences. But that'll change. *I'll* change it."

"That's *your* fantasy."

"I'll fit in, Reggie," Max promised. "You'll see. Because you're forgetting the most important thing. Anabelle's in love with me."

"Anabelle thinks you're wonderful now, and that's fine. She's even convinced her parents to say the same thing, but I think they're saying that because they don't want to hurt Anabelle. Maybe she'll stay crazy about you for a year. But it won't last forever."

"Why not?" Max said sharply. Reggie could see the anger gathering in his eyes. "What do you know about love, hotshot?"

"Not much. But that's not what I'm talking about. I'm talking about the future. Anabelle is going to marry someone from *her* background, with *her* values, and with the same wealth. Her parents have probably been telling her that all her life. It's been drummed into her. You think she's going to disobey?"

"Who's talking about marriage?" Max scoffed.

"Come on, tell me that's not your goal. After you get your foothold in Barnswell—"

"You've been reading too many novels."

"And when Anabelle gets tired of you," Reggie added, "do you really think you'll have any future here? Would you even want one?"

"Hey, why don't you just shut up," Max snapped. He got out of the chair, turning his back to Reggie, and stared out to the lake. Framed by the window, it looked dead and gray. Max turned sullenly. "I thought we were friends."

"I'm trying to be one."

"Some friend. All you do is criticize. Paint a gloomy picture."

"That's not true."

"Listen, Reggie, you think you're smarter than I am, but you've got your own problems."

"We're not talking about my problems," he said uneasily.

"Yes we are. Because it's all relevant. I finally figured you out, Reggie."

Reggie was quiet, not wanting to hear this.

"You don't believe in yourself. That's why you can't believe in me or anyone else."

Max's words stung him like arrows, sharp stabs that burned painfully inward. He struggled for something to say but all that came out was, "I'm sorry."

"Sure, Reggie. Sure you're sorry. Hey, weren't you about to leave?"

Reggie picked up his jacket and walked outside. He felt hurt and alone. Things had gotten out of control. He'd only meant to help Max. He wanted to tell him about Kenny and Hunter. He was certain that something was up. But Max probably wouldn't have listened, just called it more doom and gloom from Reggie.

In the cabin Reggie stretched out on his bunk as Max's words echoed in his head. Max really had figured him out, and Reggie had no defense. All he wanted now was to sleep. But just as he dozed off Philip stormed into the cabin, the horse face squinched in laughter.

CHAPTER 20

The slender crescent of a moon hung like a cardboard silhouette in the darkness, its lower cusp pointing to the lake. Anabelle waited patiently in her room as the creaks on the staircase informed her that her parents were on their way up. When they peeked their heads in to say good night, she gave each a kiss and pretended to go back to a book. From the crack under the door she watched the last house lights go off.

Her desk clock read twenty after ten. It had been a depressing Sunday. But after the torrent of rain, the sky had finally cleared and the air warmed a few degrees. Now her spirits were up. Anabelle threw on some jeans and a light sweater, and as an afterthought grabbed a jacket. It could get cold on the lake. She scampered down the back stairs like a mouse. A dog's barking carried across the night.

Anabelle had never felt more alive as she hurried down the street to meet Max. Sneaking out, taking risks—why hadn't she done something like this sooner? Living under Hunter's shadow, she felt like she'd missed half her life. The late-night boat ride was Max's idea, but it was something she might have thought of. The important thing was it would be fun, just she and Max gliding across the lake as if it were their own.

A pickup streaked past as Anabelle crossed the shore road. She half ran now, afraid of being late. The sand under her feet felt compressed and hard from the rain. In the distance, lit by a floodlight on a pole, three rickety quays extended into the lake like twisted fingers, their shadows vanishing into the blackness of the water. A dozen outboards, tied up at different cleats, pitched gently.

Anabelle leaned against the light pole, disappointed. It wasn't like Max to be late. What was keeping him? Listening to the water slapping against the boat hulls, she was half in a trance. When she stared at one of the motorboats, she could make out a shadowy smile of teeth across its bow.

Something stirred behind her. As Anabelle turned, a figure emerged from behind a lifeguard tower, then ducked back. Her stomach quivered. "Max?" she whispered hoarsely. When there was no answer, she took a couple of steps toward the lake.

"Who's there?" she demanded.

Slowly, the figure moved toward her. Anabelle craned her neck. As her eyes adjusted, she relaxed slightly. Hunter looked handsome in his jeans and denim jacket. Compared to the last time they'd met, his face was more confident.

"What are you doing here?" she said.

"I was just going to ask you the same thing."

"I'm waiting for someone. We're going for a walk."

"A walk. That's nice." He smiled.

"And we'd like to be alone," she said pointedly. Hunter knew it was a lie, she thought.

"Your parents know you're out here?" he asked suddenly.

"No. But if you care so much, why don't you go tell them?"

Hunter chuckled. "You're really something, Anabelle. How much longer are you going to keep covering up for Max?"

"Tell me why you're here," she said, ignoring the question.

"Okay. Why not?" He stood inches from Anabelle, taking

his time. He acted so superior. "Somebody told me you two were taking out a boat tonight. I came down to wish you *bon voyage*."

"*Who* told you?"

"Can't remember."

"Sure," she said, getting more annoyed. He was making her uncomfortable.

"I'm going to do you a favor, Anabelle. Let me walk you home."

"No thanks."

"I think it'd be a good idea."

"Why?"

"Because you don't want to go out in a boat with Max."

"What's that supposed to mean?"

"Just come with me. Let Max take a ride by himself."

"Why shouldn't I go out in the boat?" She was torn between feeling nervous and feeling angry.

"You might catch a cold," he said impatiently.

"I don't like this—"

Hunter suddenly reached for her arm, jerking her toward him. The pain caught her by surprise. Trying to free herself, Anabelle lurched back and nearly lost her balance. She expected Hunter to come after her, but when she glanced up he was sprinting toward the road. In the distance, walking from a different direction, Max's loping figure moved toward the docks.

"What's going on?" Max said. He caught a glimpse of the disappearing figure.

"It was just Hunter," she explained, relieved. She noticed that Max's eyes were bloodshot, and he was unsteady on his feet. "Are you all right?" she asked.

"Fine." He rubbed his eyes.

"Sure?"

"Just a few beers before the moonlight cruise." He wrapped his arms around her cheerfully. "Are you warm enough? You're shivering—"

"Hunter scared me."

"How?"

"He said I shouldn't go on the boat with you."

"That's all?"

"It was the way he said it. His tone—"

Max didn't seem worried. He pulled a key from his pocket and levered himself into the outboard nearest the light pole. It was a beauty, Anabelle thought, slim and low in the water, navy with a gold racing stripe along both sides. The engine looked larger than the others. Max had told her he'd taken out the boat before.

"Aren't you worried?" she asked, as he helped her in.

"Come on, you know Hunter's game. He tries to scare everyone. All bark, no bite."

"You think so?"

Max smiled reassuringly. "Who do you trust—him or me?"

"Okay," she said, dropping on the seat, but she wasn't sure. She wanted Max to promise her again, only she didn't want to sound like a coward. She watched uneasily as he twisted the pull rope around the engine and gave a clean yank. The motor purred to a start. Fine, so far. But only when Max backed the boat out from the quay did she feel more secure. The boat hadn't sunk or caught on fire. Max was probably right. Hunter was just bluffing, trying to scare her back to him.

Max guided the boat quietly away from the beach. A couple hundred yards out it picked up speed and began to pitch more wildly. Anabelle didn't mind; if anything, she liked the rough ride. She found the beer that Max said he'd stashed on board, opened a can, and sat back, closing her eyes.

Water sprayed up and coated her face in a fine mist. As Max played with the throttle, the boat jumped, jarring her from her seat. Anabelle laughed. The exhilaration was like a roller coaster.

"How do you like it?" Max yelled from the wheel.

"I love it!"

"Faster?"

"Yes!"

The boat took off like a jet, pinning her against her seat. The black water suddenly looked flat and endless. Was the earth really flat, she wondered and laughed at herself. Max guided the outboard through one figure eight, then another, until Anabelle begged him to stop.

"You're making me seasick," she said, giggling.

"Drink your beer!"

"What about the noise from the motor?"

"What about it?"

"Someone might hear us." She didn't want to spoil the fun, but part of her suddenly worried about being caught.

Max shook his head confidently. "We're too far out. Unless Fitzroy wanders down to the docks, he'll never know one of his boats is missing. And he won't check. Every night the old goat takes a warm glass of milk and drops into a coma."

They laughed together as Anabelle turned her gaze back to Barnswell. The lights continued to fade. She wanted them to disappear altogether. Barnswell represented her fears, Anabelle thought. She was tired of the routine, the boredom, the expectations that she'd always be a good little girl. There weren't enough surprises in her life. Until now, when she made her choice to date someone outside of her small Barnswell circle. She wished that Max was taking her far away and she'd never have to return.

Anabelle sat up, growing colder, and started to move next

to Max when the engine sputtered. It gave a violent, futile cough, the sound a car made when it couldn't start on a winter morning. Max jerked the throttle back and forth. The engine died with a final wheeze. "Great," Max grumbled.

"What happened?" The silence dropped around them as if they were in a solitary cell. Anabelle's eyes saw nothing but darkness.

"Probably just a spark plug," Max said, trying to sound nonchalant.

He found a flashlight under the driver's seat. Anabelle trailed behind uncertainly. Her confidence of the last few minutes, her dislike of the known, had vanished completely. She tried to control her fear but her imagination was too strong. They were in the middle of the lake, over a mile from shore, floating aimlessly. The boat had no anchor, no radio, no lights. She peered at the boat engine; it was a maze of metal and wires, and she knew nothing about it. Why hadn't she ever learned mechanics? She couldn't tell a spark plug from a piston.

"I can't find anything wrong," Max said, puzzled.

"It has to be something." Her mind flashed back to Hunter and she felt a pit opening in her stomach.

The flashlight swept silently over the engine again. After a moment, Max unscrewed the gas cap and lowered his nose. Then he shot the beam down into the tiny hole. "Empty," he said in a disbelieving voice, as if someone had just died.

Anabelle checked for herself. "Didn't you fill it with gas?" she asked.

"Late this afternoon."

"Oh no," she whispered. "Hunter . . ."

"This time I'm really going to clobber him."

"You don't know it was him," she protested weakly, hoping somehow Hunter wasn't involved.

"I can't prove it, just like with the lifeguard tower. But I know—" He removed the cushions from the rear seat and opened the storage compartment. The life jackets had been removed. "I'm going to kill him," Max swore.

Anabelle wrapped her arm through Max's. A wind lifted off the lake, cutting through her parka. "Someone will find us in the morning, won't they?" The thought suddenly cheered her.

"Sure. If you want to wait that long."

"Why not wait? I'll make it. We're together."

"Your parents are going to be pissed off," Max said suddenly. He stared toward Barnswell. "Really angry."

"I don't care what they think."

"You should," Max said. "They can make things tough for you. For us."

"I'll tell them that getting stuck out here was Hunter's fault. It's the truth, isn't it?"

"But we took the boat out."

"Still, we would have been back—"

"Forget it," Max said, frustrated. "No one's going to believe us. I'm the guy who'll catch all the blame. I'm an outsider, remember? Your father will be all over me. He won't let you see me anymore."

"I don't care what he says—"

"It's going to happen that way."

"I won't let it. Please—just sit down and we'll wait till morning."

"I can't," Max said after a pause. He peeled off his shirt.

"What are you doing?"

"I'm not going to let us get into trouble. No way." He peered at the water, leaning over the boat as he pushed in a testing hand. Then he took off his sneakers.

"Max!"

She tried to stop him, but even slightly tipsy he was too quick. His body arched into the silvery water, disappeared, and bobbed up. The lake dwarfed him like he was a minnow.

"You can't swim to shore!"

"I'm a lifeguard, remember? Of course I can swim."

"What are you going to do?"

"Get another boat. Then I'll come back for you. Signal me with the flashlight. I'll tow you in. No sweat," he added almost cheerily.

"You're crazy!"

"You want to spend the whole night out here? You want to face your father in the morning?"

"Max, it's a whole mile. After a while the water will get too cold."

"I don't think we have a choice," he said, suddenly impatient. "I have to make it. Can't you understand that?"

She wanted to say yes, but there were other considerations. Max's safety was only one. She didn't want to be left alone. She wished she were braver, but she wasn't and the thought of drifting helplessly in a boat that might or might not hold up till morning was terrifying.

"Please stay," she asked.

"I can't."

"I need you."

"Anabelle, it's our necks," Max said. And then he was gone, an iridescent speck plodding toward distant lights.

CHAPTER 21

The numbness started in his legs and slowly spread toward his chest. Max could feel the wind on his face, but everything below the water was anesthetized. His hatred for Hunter kept his hands and feet paddling, slow, determined strokes that propelled him toward shore. If anything should happen to Anabelle in that boat, Max thought, Hunter's ass was grass. Max had lost sight of Anabelle and the outboard long ago, yet the town lights still looked tiny and insignificant. He had figured the swim to take no more than an hour. Maybe the beer was slowing him down; he felt he'd been in the lake half the night.

His head suddenly dipped and his mouth filled with water. Max gagged as he thrashed around. Come on, he thought, spitting out the water, you can make it. A little farther. He'd survived football games on sweltering afternoons, hiked the tallest mountains in the Alleghenies, raced a bicycle a hundred miles—what was a little night swim?

But his strength was ebbing. He fantasized he was in a swimming pool, churning out laps, the pool wall always within reach. Only there was no wall. His hand scooped up more water. Tired, so tired. For the first time this summer, for the first time he could remember, he began to doubt himself. Maybe he wasn't such a great athlete. Maybe there were things that desire alone couldn't accomplish. How good a swimmer could he be? What if he didn't reach the shore? For a moment he stopped, treading water, surveying the endless expanse of black lake. The thought of drowning chilled him.

Max doggedly stretched one hand over his head, then the other, fighting the water. Someone shouted his name. Jerking his head up, he looked around frantically. Nobody was there. Was he going crazy? He flipped on his back to conserve strength, but all that did was to make him dizzy. Sleepy, too. The lake was like a bed, a cold silk sheet that wrapped around him.

Come on, he told himself again, you can do it. You *have* to do it.

But he wondered who he was talking to.

CHAPTER 22

Curled on his bunk, Reggie studied the luminous dial of his watch. After midnight already, and Max wasn't back. Sunday night the town closed down early, so maybe he was at Anabelle's, but that would be pushing it with Mr. and Mrs. Livingston. Then where? Reggie knew better than to worry, but something stuck in his mind. Seeing Kenny with Hunter this afternoon. And tonight, just before dinner, he had spotted Hunter again, alone, strolling near the docks. The beach was cold and deserted—so what was he up to?

Reggie had waited all evening to apologize to Max. When he didn't show for dinner, Reggie combed the town unsuccessfully. He rose now from his bed and listened to the cicadas. The symphony came every night, a high-pitched but tender lullaby that usually relaxed him. Tonight it kept him awake. Across the cabin, Kenny slept on his back with his mouth open, his chest jerking with every breath. The eyelids fluttered.

Reggie reached over and shook him.

As Kenny lurched up he looked frightened. Only when he focused on Reggie did his breathing slow. "What?" he said, frowning. Reggie put a finger to his lips and motioned him into the latrine.

"What do you want?" he asked, still sleepy. He shielded his eyes as Reggie flicked on the john lights.

"Do you know where Max is?"

Kenny pondered the question, as if there might be another answer than a simple yes or no. "Why?" he said.

"He didn't come back tonight." Kenny looked bemused.

"I saw you and Hunter at the pub," Reggie prodded. "What were you talking about?"

"It was mostly Hunter talking," Kenny said defensively. "I just listened."

"What did he want?"

A sigh of resignation came from Kenny's lips. He twisted on a faucet and splashed water up to his face, staring at Reggie through the mirror. "Hunter warned me not to tell anyone. But I guess I will. I don't hate Max, he's just too pushy sometimes."

"Tell what?" said Reggie, growing more anxious.

"It all started with the fire. I was around the beach when the tower went up. A lot of people saw me. The next day Hunter said the police were investigating the fire, and that I was a prime suspect. I couldn't believe it. I mean, all I was doing was taking a walk."

"So?" Reggie wished he'd hurry up with his story.

"Hunter kept asking me to meet him at the pub. When I finally did, he tried to blackmail me. He said that unless I got Max and you guys to quit as lifeguards, he'd tell the police chief he saw me start the fire. He said the chief was a good friend of his father's."

"What did you do?"

"Nothing. I was scared, but I decided that Hunter could do what he wanted. I knew I hadn't started the fire, and I resented being intimidated. I think Hunter knew that. Because, all of a sudden, he changed his tune.

"The next time we met he came across as real buddy-buddy. He wanted to be my friend. He wanted to be everyone's friend, including Max. It was time to make peace, he said. He was especially sorry for badmouthing Max so much. I admitted that Philip and I had done a little of that, too. It was all wrong, we agreed, and we should make it up to Max. At the pub this afternoon, Hunter suggested I go drinking with Max tonight. Show him a good time. Get him really sloshed. That would make up for the damage."

"Did you?" Reggie asked.

"No way. The whole idea sounded phony. I told Hunter I didn't like to drink. When he heard that, he gave me the cold shoulder and walked away."

"But why get Max drunk?" Reggie said.

Kenny looked disgusted. "Go ask Philip."

"Philip?" Reggie didn't get it.

"He's the one who did it. Came across as Max's good buddy. Just like Hunter wanted him too."

Reggie's skin turned clammy. Rushing back to the beds he seized Philip by the shoulders as he slept. You spoiled preppy, thought Reggie. Max was right. You're one of them. Philip's sad face twitched uncomfortably with a second shake. Finally the eyes popped open like a doll's, dull and rheumy.

"Where's Max?" Reggie demanded.

Philip was puzzled, but then he chuckled. "I get it. You're Max's little brother. You're worried."

"Tell me!"

"It was just a joke, Reggie. Cool it."

"Getting him drunk?"

"Yeah. That was part of it. So what? No harm, no foul."

"You better explain—"

"Hey, watch your tone, huh? Don't get pissed at me. All I know was Max was going out on a boat tonight. He got the key from the goofy kid, Roger, the one who runs the docks. Roger happens to be a friend of Hunter's, and he snitched on Max. You get it now?"

"No," Reggie said impatiently.

Philip rolled his eyes, as if he didn't believe how dense Reggie could be. "Hunter guessed that with Max drunk and all, he'd make a real racket when he went for the boat. Hunter was going to tip off the hotel. Fitzroy would come down and catch him in the act. Fire him on the spot, probably." He looked at Reggie. "Hey, don't look so surprised. Max had it coming, the big peacock."

"And that's supposed to be the joke?" Reggie said.

"Yeah."

"You're a traitor."

Philip gave a smirk. "I got news for you, Reggie. Max was all over your case tonight. After a few beers, he said you were the world's biggest phony. Now how do you feel?"

Reggie tried to control himself. His instinct was to drag Philip onto the floor and ram a fist down his mouth, but there wasn't time. "Did Hunter call Fitzroy?"

"I guess," Philip allowed.

"Then why wasn't Max caught? Why isn't he back in the cabin?"

Philip shrugged innocently. "Got me."

"When did you see Max last?"

"Ten-thirty or so."

Reggie fumbled into his clothes. "Let's go," he said to Philip. "And bring a flashlight."

"Hey, pal, it's the middle of the night."

"You got Max into trouble," Reggie said, "and now you're going to help get him out."

In the near-moonless night the beach looked ghostly and forgotten. Reggie hurried toward the lone floodlight by the docks. The blue outboard was missing. Max was either still out on the lake, Reggie calculated, or the boat had been moored somewhere else. He told Philip to start walking along the shore. If he found the boat without Max, he was to keep searching. Philip's eyes wandered over the lake. For the first time he seemed worried.

"You really think something happened to Max?" he asked as he folded his arms.

"Maybe."

"I didn't know what Hunter was up to. Honest," he swore, as if suddenly realizing how badly Hunter had duped him.

"Forget that now. Let's go."

"I just want you to know I'm sorry."

A rowboat bobbed up at the end of one quay. Reggie jumped in with the flashlight, slid the oars into place, and headed out. The squeal of the oarlocks was like a fingernail traveling down a blackboard.

Reggie's arms moved smartly in rotation, but the blades of the oars continually hit at the wrong angle, too deep or too shallow. Frustrated, he rowed faster. Water still splashed up around him. The air was cold. He steered in a straight line from the docks, an arbitrary direction, but anything tonight would be a guess. A pain began to burn in his forearms and biceps. As he grew more tired, he braced his feet against the hull for support and kept rowing. Resting wasn't permitted. When he was about half a mile out, Barnswell began to blur behind him as if wrapped in a fog.

"Max!" He shouted into the void as he held up the oars momentarily. "Max!"

Not even an echo. He went back to rowing, twisting his head around every half minute to search the immense, dark wilderness of water. How could anyone be out there? Every minute Max's name came off his lips in a deep, breathless roar. Whenever the silence returned he felt absurd, that he could be here all night and find nothing. Maybe Max wasn't even on the lake. Maybe he was at Anabelle's after all. Please, let it be, thought Reggie. He pulled out the flashlight. The beam jumped over the lake but with mixed results. The light was faint at a distance over fifty feet, and even closer in it seemed to bounce off the water rather than penetrate it.

Then he heard something. A faint, hopeless thrashing. Reggie pulled in the oars and slowly raised himself up in the boat. The flashlight swept over the water again.

Max was floating face down. His bare back looked pale and spongy. No, Reggie thought, trembling, it couldn't be.

He leaned over the bow, frozen in indecision. On instinct he plunged in with his clothes on. His arms chopped through the water without feeling. Faster, he thought. When he reached the body he jerked Max's head up.

Reggie wondered if he was dead. The body felt warm, a good sign, but the eyes were tightly shut. Yet Reggie had heard movement in the water, or thought he had. He suddenly shook Max by the shoulders, as if to wake him from a slumber. Nothing. Prying open the jaw, he wormed a finger into Max's mouth. Water trickled out.

There was probably more in his lungs, but how much? First he had to get Max to the boat. He hated himself for having jumped out. Stupid. Not thinking. The rowboat was already drifting. Reggie braced an arm under Max's chin, turning him on his back, his face up for air. With his free hand, Reggie paddled frantically toward the boat.

It was like towing an anchor. Max's weight and inertia pulled Reggie under twice. His muscles were on fire again. He remembered how he'd once tried to lift Max, drunk and asleep, from one bunk to another, and that he'd given up quickly. Now he couldn't give up. Not on Max. Not on himself either. He kicked desperately, guiding his hand through the silvery water.

The boat was getting closer. Reggie tried to ignore his

pain, but when his hand finally touched the hull he was exhausted. He took a breath. The difficult part was still ahead.

He readjusted his hold on Max, moving behind him. One at a time, he lifted Max's hands onto the lip of the boat, curling them over the edge, as if they might grab hold. Stay, just for a minute, Reggie begged, as he pulled himself up into the boat. Before he was halfway in, Max's hands fell free. He plunged back into the lake like a slippery log. Reggie dived after him.

He began to worry as he pulled Max up. With every second Max seemed to grow heavier and Reggie weaker. His legs had turned numb; his arms were rubber.

It suddenly occurred to Reggie that Max might drown him before it was over.

Dazed, he focused on the oarlock above him. It was horseshoe shaped, with the opening at the top. Maybe, just maybe, he thought. Max's right hand came up and Reggie forced the wrist through the oarlock opening. It fit as snugly as if locked in a handcuff. So far, so good. Now stay there, Reggie prayed. As Max dangled from the hull by one arm, Reggie moved to the other side of the boat, to keep it balanced. With an effort he pulled himself on board. He looked up breathlessly, hoping. Max was still hanging there.

Reggie wrung the water off his hands and stumbled toward his friend, seizing the limp arm. The boat lurched sharply and Reggie dropped hard on one knee. When he picked himself up, he spread his legs for stability and lifted again. He thought his back would snap. His whole body was trembling.

As if someone were pushing from below, Max's head and neck slowly rode up over the bow. Reggie was startled. I can do it, he thought. I know I can do it. His adrenaline was pumping now. He leaned over Max, getting a good grip on his left leg. The boat pitched violently to one side, threatening to capsize. Reggie held on. Imperceptibly, Max's leg came up, stiff and extended, an inch at a time. Finally, the body rested on the lip of the bow. Then, with a sharp tug from Reggie, Max crashed to the bottom of the boat.

Reggie rested only for a second. He had to be quick now. Turning Max on his back, Reggie pinched his nostrils closed. He pressed his mouth down, forcing his breath into Max's lungs, backed off a moment, and repeated the technique. He'd done it a dozen times when Max's head suddenly turned. Please, Reggie thought, breathe. He put his ear closer. A wheeze came from Max's nose. Come on, keep it up. Reggie flipped Max over and straddled his back.

Pushing on Max's shoulders, he then lifted the upper arms, and quickly leaned down on the shoulders again. Like any good lifeguard would do. Waiting for the water to empty from his lungs. Pushing down again. And waiting.

CHAPTER 23

The ambulance siren had pierced Reggie's consciousness, refusing to leave it even after Max was brought to the hospital. He would always remember it, a lonely, plaintive cry. Sitting in the hospital hallway, Reggie wondered if the night would ever end. He could still see himself in the rowboat, struggling, wondering if he'd ever get Max back to shore. Reggie had made the rescue despite his own doubts. Inside his head his own solitary voice had broken through to tell him that Max could not be allowed to die. Reggie had listened and believed in himself. He had rowed back to the docks without resting, run to the hotel to phone, and waited for the ambulance.

The Barnswell hospital, a small stucco building not far from the hotel, provided the town with an emergency room, inpatient beds, a single operating room, and a pharmacy. Several nurses were on duty around the clock, and local doctors came when needed. An internist had been examining Max for almost an hour. With oxygen, he had regained consciousness in the ambulance, but he had blacked out again.

"Coffee?" a nurse asked, approaching Reggie. She was pretty, he noticed. Taking the Styrofoam cup, he asked how Max was, but she didn't know.

At least Anabelle was all right. The hotel watchman had dispatched two search boats when Reggie reported what happened. They found Anabelle curled up on the seat of the blue outboard, cold and afraid, but unharmed. Reggie was relieved when he heard. He had guessed that Anabelle was on the boat, but with Max in trouble there'd been no time to search. Reggie was more distressed by what the search team hadn't found. There was no gas in the engine, no extra gas can on board, and no life jackets. Max took chances, but he wasn't careless.

Through the window Reggie watched the sky lighten and its edges turn a soft pink. He suddenly felt his exhaustion, as if with the coming of daylight the last traces of his adrenaline were gone. A doctor approached with a stethoscope dangling from his neck.

"I checked your friend out thoroughly," he announced to Reggie. The doctor was in his fifties, salt-and-pepper hair, thick glasses. The voice was businesslike but caring. "There's no brain damage from oxygen loss. I think you got to him just in time. But his lungs are still weak. And he's exhausted and disoriented. I want to keep him in for observation at least a couple days. Maybe a week."

"Can I see him?"

"He's sleeping. Why don't you come back this afternoon?"

"Sure." Reggie felt his whole body relax. He thanked the doctor for the good news. Max would be all right after all. *I think you got to him just in time.* Reggie had tapped a source of confidence that he never knew he had, and he felt good. He felt good about himself. Maybe he wasn't such a loser after all.

As Reggie approached the hotel Philip waved from the veranda. Reggie quickened his pace. Beyond, the lake looked warm and tranquil, as if the events of the night had never happened.

"How is he?" asked Philip anxiously.

"He'll be okay. He can't have visitors yet."

Philip looked thankful. "I told everyone in the cabin what happened. They really appreciate what you did."

"It's okay."

"They also want to string up Hunter from the nearest telephone pole."

It would never happen, Reggie knew, suddenly angry. No one could pin anything on Hunter, just like with the tower fire. Hunter was too clever. "Have you heard anything from Fitzroy?"

"Not yet. But my guess is he's furious. The night watchman told him everything."

Reggie ducked into the hotel. Early risers were already shuffling into the dining room, lured by the aroma of fried bacon and butter-rich pastries. Reggie took a chance and scampered up the stairs to the mezzanine. Fitzroy's secretary hadn't arrived, but the inner door was ajar.

"Mr. Fitzroy?" Reggie called, knocking on the glass door.

The hotel manager looked up crossly, as if the interruption displeased him, and peered quizzically at Reggie. "Aren't you a lifeguard?" he said.

"I wanted to explain what happened last night."

"You mean with Mr. Riley?"

"He didn't intend to hurt anyone. What happened—"

"He broke hotel rules," Fitzroy interrupted. "He jeopardized property. He endangered lives. Legally, he put the whole hotel at risk." His anger was building quickly.

"I understand," Reggie said. "But there were special circumstances."

"You mean excuses."

Reggie wondered how he should bring up Hunter. Fitzroy might think it was trying to shift the blame, yet he wanted to give him the real picture. "Not exactly excuses."

"I don't care what you tell me. Max Riley is no longer employed by this hotel. The Sherborne will cover his medical bills, but as of this moment he's fired. If I'd listened to Mr. Carlton, I would have dismissed him weeks ago."

Arguing was futile. Reggie retreated downstairs, shaken. Maybe he should have anticipated Fitzroy's reaction, but he'd been too caught up in the events of the night. Who had time to think of the future? But as he ate his breakfast in the kitchen, Reggie began to think. He was headed toward Anabelle's house before eight.

"Morning," Reggie said awkwardly when Mrs. Livingston came to the door. She was in her robe and looked tired. She didn't look happy to see visitors.

"I came to find out how Anabelle was doing," Reggie explained, trying to break her cold manner.

"She's resting, thank you. Poor foolish thing. She was frightened to death. Is Max all right?"

Reggie nodded. "The doctors want him in the hospital for a while." He coughed into his fist. "Mrs. Livingston, do you mind if I come in?"

She hesitated, as if trying to decide what Reggie wanted, or what it would accomplish to invite him inside. "All right. Just for a minute."

Reggie could hear a shower running upstairs. He sat on the edge of a couch, feeling not entirely welcome, and gave his speech. He was doing this for Max, and to clear the air. "I wanted to tell you that Max never intended for anything to happen last night. It was supposed to be fun, taking the boat out."

"Anabelle should never have gone off with him," Mrs Livingston replied. "It wasn't like her. I don't know why she did it. But she'll be punished."

Reggie waited for Mrs. Livingston to add that Max should

be punished, too, but she held back. "Would it be possible to talk to Anabelle?" he asked.

"It's not a good time now."

"Maybe later, when she feels up to it?"

"I'll have to speak with her father first."

"I know that Max is sorry. You know how he feels about Anabelle. He really cares for her."

"I gather," she answered, but she didn't seem to believe it. The shower suddenly turned off, and the silence closed around them. Mrs. Livingston glanced to the door. "Thank you for coming by, Reggie. It was thoughtful of you to ask about Anabelle."

"Max just made a mistake," Reggie said as he rose. "It happens to everybody."

"Of course," she said.

"What I really wanted to tell you," Reggie spoke up, struggling, "was getting stuck on the lake wasn't entirely Max's fault."

"Then whose fault was it?" she asked.

"I think someone deliberately emptied most of the gas from the engine. Someone wanted them to stall in the middle of the lake." Reggie wondered if he had to spell it out. Mrs. Livingston could guess.

"I'll tell Anabelle you were by, Reggie," she said, turning away.

Mr. Livingston appeared in his robe, looking hardly rested or calm. He glanced once at Reggie, his face stern and unforgiving, and moved silently toward the kitchen. Reggie felt a chill as he turned to leave. Max had called Mr. Livingston a nice guy. Sure he was. And Joe DiMaggio played fullback for the New York Jets.

CHAPTER 24

Flowers. Reggie hated them. They reminded him of his father's funeral. But on his lunch break he bought a bunch of cut mums and daisies and walked to the hospital. Maybe Max would be up. The linoleum tiles squeaked under his feet as a nurse directed him down a sun-splashed corridor. Max was sitting in hospital pajamas and a light cotton robe, looking subdued. The corner room had a view of the Sherborne.

"Hey, Max—" Reggie called cheerfully, holding up the flowers.

Max turned with a start. They looked at one another, not quite sure what to say. Finally, Max put the flowers on the bedside table and smiled moodily. "Well, here I am. Still breathing."

"For a fish, you don't look so bad."

"Sure. Just a little waterlogged," Max replied. He looked embarrassed about what had happened. "Thanks for pulling me out last night," he managed.

"You would have done the same for me."

"Yeah. Except you wouldn't have been dumb enough to take out a boat in the middle of the night."

"Don't be so hard on yourself. It was Hunter who screwed you."

"It's strange," Max admitted. "I'm not even pissed off at the worm. I'm mad at myself for letting my guard down. I should have anticipated. Ever since I woke up I've been thinking about that. It was my fault."

"It could have happened to anyone."

Max shook his head in disbelief. "Maybe you can tell me what went wrong last night."

"You don't remember?"

"Oh, I remember all right," Max said. "The boat. Anabelle. Running out of gas. Then I jumped into the water. What I want to know is, why couldn't I make it to shore?"

"You were drunk. And exhausted."

Max considered the explanation, but he wasn't convinced. "I can't believe I didn't make it," he said.

"Listen, the night's over. Forget it."

He sighed. "Maybe you're right. Who cares anyway, huh?" he said, cheering himself up. "I was careless, but I won't be anymore." He opened his closet, and grimaced at a pair of still damp jeans. "Reggie, I need some clothes."

"What for?"

"What do you mean what for? I'm splitting."

"The doctor wants you here for observation."

"So I'll come back." Max flashed a cocky grin. "Look at me, will you? Have you ever seen me more healthy? I could swim the whole lake and back if I had to now. Besides, I've got to pay a visit."

"If you mean Anabelle—"

"Look, you know I have to smooth things over," Max said, determined.

Reggie dropped on the foot of Max's bed, thinking it was better to tell him now than later. "I was at her house this morning. Anabelle was resting—she's okay, though. I spoke to her mother. She wasn't too pleased with what happened."

"Tell me about it. I called Anabelle an hour ago. Mrs.

Livingston wouldn't even put her on the phone. Anabelle was being punished, she said. I told her it wasn't her fault."

"Maybe you should lay low for a while," Reggie suggested. "Let things cool down."

"No way. I have to see Anabelle—right now."

"Anabelle's parents are really mad," Reggie repeated himself, but Max wasn't listening again.

"So they're upset. They'll forgive and forget in time. Maybe I won't be working at the store right away. No sweat. I'll finish the summer as a lifeguard. The important thing is that I see Anabelle."

"Well, about the beach," Reggie interrupted gently. Max cocked his head, waiting. "It's over. They won't take you back."

"What?"

"Fitzroy fired you this morning."

"Fired *me?*" he said, incredulous. "Without giving me a chance to explain? Come on. What's going on—"

"I talked to Fitzroy. It didn't do any good." Reggie wondered why he had to be the one to give the bad news. "You had to know it was coming."

Max flopped on the bed. He spread his open fingers over his face like a mask, deliberating. "All right. Maybe I'll stick with the store after all."

"You just said that wasn't going to work."

"I'll make it work!"

Reggie didn't know how to deal with this side of Max. Here he was again, planning a new strategy. Max wanted to see the lake incident as a minor setback, nothing more. Reggie had hoped that somehow the experience would have finally made him see that he didn't belong in Barnswell. Getting back in the Livingstons' good graces was hopeless.

Max had to be a real masochist. "Did you ever think of going back to Bradley for the rest of the summer?" Reggie suggested.

"And do what?"

"Make a clean start. It's almost time for school. Finish up, then head out to California next year, like you always planned."

"You mean leave Anabelle?" he said. "Here you go again. You're a broken record, Reggie."

"I think you'd do great in California."

"Give it up, Reggie. I have a place in Barnswell. Last night it may have been jeopardized, but I didn't lose it."

Reggie could feel Max's determination. It was irreversible, like a tide sweeping toward shore, covering everything in its path. In a way Reggie couldn't help rooting for him. Yet his doubts were as strong as ever.

"Reggie, how about running back and bringing me fresh clothes now," Max ordered.

Reggie looked away for a moment, summoning his courage. It was so hard to stand up to Max.

"No," he said.

"I didn't hear you, Harrison."

"I'm not going to do it. If you want clothes, get them yourself."

"What are you pulling?—"

"You're weak. You need to stay and rest. I'm not going to spring you and be responsible if you collapse a few hours from now."

"Rest?" he echoed. "How can I rest when I've got all this on my mind?"

"You'll find a way."

"Sorry, I'm getting out—"

Reggie raised his voice. "You try it and I'll tell the duty

nurse. As far as I'm concerned they can put a guard on the door."

Max glared back, furious, and maybe a little hurt, thought Reggie. He looked exhausted, and suddenly Max, as if knowing it, settled back on his bed for a moment. "Maybe I'll stay for one more day," he conceded. "But only if you help me, Reggie," he threatened.

"Help you what?"

"I'm going to write Anabelle a letter. She's my only hope. Her parents' feelings don't really matter. I have to convince her I'm sorry. My mistake was leaving the boat. She's holding that against me, I know it." He shut his eyes, as if reliving the scene.

"What makes you think a letter's going to work?" said Reggie.

"I know Anabelle like a book. She didn't think I was a hero swimming to shore. She thought I was deserting her to save face. And she was right. You know what was really going through my mind? That I'd been outsmarted by Hunter. I wasn't going to to give him the satisfaction of seeing me stranded in the middle of the lake. It was too humiliating. That's why I swam for shore."

From his bedside table, Max pulled out some paper that read BARNSWELL HEALTH SERVICES, and curled over it with a quiet determination. He wrote spontaneously, compulsively, without lifting the pen from the paper. In twenty minutes he had covered three sheets on all sides, endless blue swirls asking for forgiveness and acceptance. Max folded the letter crisply into an envelope.

"Take it," Max ordered.

"I think you're wasting your time."

"Fine, Reggie. I'll pop over to the Livingstons' in my pajamas and see Anabelle myself."

Reluctantly, Reggie tucked the envelope in his pocket. It was all *déjà vu*. He had been Max's go-between before with the business letter to Anabelle's father. "But what if I can't get into the house? I mean, I've been there, and if her parents are still around . . ."

"Just wait till they're out," Max said simply.

"What am I supposed to do—stand lookout?"

"Don't be dumb." Max motioned for Reggie to throw him his pants. His hand snaked into a soggy pocket and extracted a single key.

"I can't break in," Reggie protested, catching the key on the fly.

"This is an emergency. They're making me do this. Just sneak in and drop the letter in Anabelle's room. The point is I have to get her the letter. It's my only shot. Are you with me or not?"

As Reggie slipped out of the hospital the letter in his pocket felt as heavy as a brick. He couldn't wait to get rid of it. He walked quickly to Anabelle's house, but two cars were in the drive. Voices drifted out from open windows. He retreated to the beach, and after dinner tried again. Most of the house lights were out, the cars gone. He rang the doorbell uncertainly, wondering what he'd say if anyone but Anabelle opened the door. There was no answer after five rings.

Reggie moved to the back door, slipped the key into the lock, and listened for the metallic click. The door popped open. His heart began to pound and his throat went dry as he stepped over the threshold. "Hello?" he called, but not very forcefully. If he were caught, he would claim the door was open. The silence wrapped around him as he drifted toward the stairs. He called Anabelle's name. Nothing. Ahead, he saw a door was open. The room looked like a girl's—

soft, pink wallpaper, a fluffy comforter on the bed. A desk lamp threw a shadow over a rocker. Quickly, Reggie propped Max's letter against a fat dictionary and took the stairs down two at a time.

As he hurried out through the living room he turned toward a plate-glass window, startled by his own reflection. He stopped, looking again. His glance took in the familiar barbecue, then rested on the two figures behind it. An outdoor floodlight cast a soft tint on Hunter and Anabelle. They were sitting across from one another, talking quietly. Reggie was in shock. How had they gotten together if Anabelle was being punished? Even if her parents weren't home, how could she let Hunter into her house? After what he'd done to the boat . . .

An outrage began to swell in Reggie, along with a demand for an explanation. Someone would have to tell him. Someone would have to tell Max. He edged closer to the window, wanting to hear them, when his foot wrapped around an electrical cord. He tried to free himseslf but the lamp teetered precariously, and when he lunged to save it, the table underneath toppled. The lamp exploded on impact.

Reggie stumbled toward the door and kept running. He was out of breath when he got to the hotel grounds. In his cabin he splashed water on his face, then slipped out of his clothes. He worried that Anabelle would call the police, but maybe, if she found Max's letter, she'd realize that Max, or even Reggie, was the intruder. Only what if Hunter discovered the letter first? Reggie tried not to think about the consequences as he pulled back his covers. On the next bunk Washington and Tiny hovered over a deck of cards, slapping them down with mock aggression. Philip had his radio earphones on, eyes half closed. Kenny was reading one of Reggie's paperbacks.

"What time are visiting hours tomorrow?" Washington said to Reggie.

"Noon to four."

"We've all chipped in for a present," Tiny put in. "A big teddy bear. No, just kidding. Four pounds of chocolate. He'll love it."

"How are his spirits?" Philip asked Reggie.

"He's a little moody. You know, he misses Anabelle," he answered ambiguously. There was no point in broadcasting Max's problems.

"Absence makes the heart grow fonder," Tiny quoted, as he produced a can of beer from under his bunk. "But old Max will be back in action soon enough."

"We want him back on the beach, too," Kenny said. "Fitzroy can lump it."

Reggie turned his eyes away from the light. Everyone was expecting miracles. He would have to tell Max in the morning, along with the news about Hunter.

CHAPTER 25

"*Hunter!* Hunter was in Anabelle's house? You're sure? What for?" Furious, Max sat up shakily in his bed. "What were they talking about?"

"I couldn't hear them" Reggie admitted. "I knocked over a lamp by accident and ran out."

Max pushed away his sheets and dropped his feet on the floor. The angle of the morning sun produced a sharp glare on the window. He was still exhausted from having awakened a little after midnight. It felt then like a pillow had been clamped over his face, like he was drowning again. He'd been given oxygen, which had helped some, and he thought he was better, but in the morning he'd almost blacked out while washing up. The internist had examined him and warned that his lungs were still weak. He ran a risk of collapsing if he overexerted himself; even emotional excitement could be dangerous. Sage advice, Max thought, but a little difficult to follow after Reggie's bombshell.

"I can't believe it," Max announced, totally frustrated. It was maddening to be stuck in the hospital.

"Maybe Hunter just came by to see how she was feeling," Reggie offered.

"Right," Max scoffed.

"I'll try and find out."

"Forget it. I just want to know if Anabelle's read my letter. You sure you put it in a conspicuous place?"

"On top of her desk."

"Then why hasn't she called me?" Max demanded.

"Well, Anabelle is . . ." Reggie tried to think of the word, "evasive, I guess. You said so yourself."

"Maybe."

"Or she's thinking over what you wrote."

"How long's that supposed to take? A year?" Max hurled a magazine across the room. "I tried calling her again. Her mother said she wasn't home. Sure."

"You have to be patient," said Reggie.

"I just can't take all this sitting around—" He grabbed a handful of stationery and began another letter. He knew the problem. Anabelle still didn't believe he was sorry for thinking of himself ahead of her. He had to convince her. Maybe he wasn't exactly Shakespeare, but he could write well enough if he tried. In his heart of hearts he really was sorry. He wasn't trying to lay on a phony apology. He meant it. The words came sluggishly at first, but then his thoughts flowed. He loved her, he wrote, more than anything else, and she had to give him the chance to prove it. She had to believe in him again, believe in the future, *their* future. Max felt his confidence growing.

"I'll deliver it," Reggie promised when Max had finished, "but I don't want to break into the house again."

"I don't care what you do. Just make sure she gets it. Reggie, I'm counting on you."

"I know."

"Find out what she thought of my first letter. And ask if she'll visit me."

"Okay."

"Don't look so glum. It's going to be all right, Reggie. I mean, haven't I always been lucky? Haven't I always got what I wanted?"

Reggie half waved good-bye. Max nestled back on the bed, thinking how much he hated the hospital. He was a prisoner again, just like at the hotel, but in a matter of days he'd be out of this dungeon and with Anabelle again. Everything would be okay. It had to be.

All he had left of his summer was Anabelle. The prestige of being a lifeguard and the victory of landing a job with Mr. Livingston were gone; he had no choice but to accept that. But Anabelle—she was someone he couldn't lose. She stood for everything he wanted. Nothing in his life had brought him so much pleasure. Was he being too ambitious to think he could keep her? Reggie thought he was in over his head, but then Reggie didn't know what it was to have a dream. Dreams were for coming true—and keeping you alive.

CHAPTER 26

Anabelle kissed her parents good-bye at the door, cleared the breakfast dishes more from habit than ambition, and settled back in a patio chair with a glass of orange juice. She watched below as the beach crowd began to mushroom. A couple of outboards rippled innocently over the calm water, followed by shrieks of laughter. It was hard to believe the summer season had only a couple of weeks to run. Anabelle's father had ended her confinement and restored her freedom after two days, but she found herself staying at home anyway. There was nowhere she particularly wanted to go. After her experience in the boat, the lake and beach made her uncomfortable.

Anabelle still didn't understand what had happened that night. She'd panicked, completely falling apart after Max had started his swim to shore. She knew, rationally, that she probably wasn't in great danger, yet her imagination had taken over, driving her into private nightmares. She'd screamed in the darkness until her voice gave out. Then she'd dropped in the boat and covered her head, as if to hide from someone. That she'd collapsed so quickly still puzzled and embarrassed her.

After the rescue her mother had been supportive and understanding, but her father acted betrayed, as if he'd been hurt and embarrassed even more than his daughter. After all, the whole town was talking. Anabelle had argued with him bitterly. She thought he was selfish for thinking of his image in the community. What about her feelings? Didn't they count for something? Her mother consoled her and tried to make Anabelle see her father's point of view. "Your father's family has been in Barnswell for generations," her mother repeated. "He values our reputation. For you and a strange boy to be joyriding in a boat reflects on him, don't you see? It's just not right . . ."

After moping, Anabelle thought over what had been said. Feeling guilty, she apologized to her father.

"I accept," he said. "But I also want you to know, young lady, that you went too far this summer. Don't play with fire and we all won't get burned." Then he gave her a forgiving kiss. He spared her the names and instances of her bad judgment, but she knew. She didn't regret falling for Max, nor the good times together. Had it really been bad judgment? Though the boat ride skirted disaster, it had started out as fun. She didn't hold anything against Max. Yet whenever she thought about him in the hospital, as much as she wanted to be with him, something kept her away. It was more than her father's wishes, but she wasn't sure what it was.

The doorbell brought Anabelle to her feet. She half expected another visit from Hunter, but when she saw Reggie she wasn't disappointed. He carried another letter in his hand.

"Come on in," she said warmly. "How's Max?"

"He's going to be all right."

"Mom said he has to stay in the hospital."

"For a few more days."

"But nothing serious—"

"No," he assured her, handing over the letter. For a moment he stared at the trunk and two suitcases near the stairs. "Somebody going on a trip?" he asked.

"Mother's so organized she's two weeks ahead of herself," Anabelle answered. "I visit my aunt in Baltimore, then take the train to school. Summer is over for me."

They sat on the patio, looking off at the mountains, and made small talk for a few minutes. Anabelle skimmed Max's letter. Poor Max. He was apologizing again, just like in the first letter, practically beating his breast. Or was it beating his head in frustration? She felt for him. She sensed Reggie was watching her carefully as she read, hoping her face would give him some clues to report back to Max. Anabelle understood. Reggie was just trying to be a friend, and she admired him for that. There should be more friends in the world like Reggie, she thought. He was someone you could talk to without fear of being preached at. Hunter, Max, her parents—they always had a point of view to ram home.

"Would you like something to eat?" Anabelle offered, when she put down the letter.

"No thanks. I have to get back." His eyes jumped impatiently to the beach. "Max was anxious to know if you'd read his other letter."

"Were you the one who brought it?"

Reggie had a hard time meeting her eyes. "I'm sorry about the lamp. I shouldn't have come in your house."

"It's all right. The lamp wasn't a really valuable one," I told Mom I broke it," she said. "Tell Max I read his letter, a couple of times in fact. It was sweet." Anabelle dropped her hands on her knees, leaning forward. "Please tell him I accept his apology, but it wasn't really necessary. I know

Max had to swim to shore. He didn't think he had a choice. And I know he did it for me as well as himself."

Reggie seemed relieved that she wasn't angry or upset. "Are you going to visit Max?" he asked.

She hesitated. "Sometime soon."

"When?"

"I don't know."

"Why don't you know?" His voice was slightly hurt, as if it were him she was disappointing.

"I haven't sorted things out in my head. Please tell Max I miss him, but I want to think about our relationship. I don't want to force anything."

"What's there to think about?" Reggie persisted. "Is there something else? Or do you mean Hunter? Maybe it's none of my business," he went on, "but I was wondering what he was doing at your house."

"Oh," she said, surprised. Reggie must have seen him when he delivered Max's letter. "He just came over to talk. He regretted what happened this summer. Setting the tower on fire, being mean to you. He also admitted emptying the gas from the boat."

Reggie looked astounded. "He confessed? And what did you say?"

"I forgave him."

Reggie could only stare in disbelief. "What?"

"He was sincere. I know Hunter."

"I don't believe this," he whispered.

Anabelle shifted in her chair, suddenly feeling uneasy. Why was Reggie doing this to her? He was supposed to be open, someone to talk to, and instead he made her feel confused and even guilty. "Look," she said, "I know Hunter acted like a spoiled child this summer, throwing tantrums when things went against him. But it was partly my fault. He thought I dumped him for Max, and that wasn't exactly easy to take. He was in shock. People under stress don't behave rationally."

"If he's so sorry for everything," Reggie spoke up, "then why doesn't he come and tell me or Max? We're the ones he hurt."

"Maybe he will."

"Oh, sure," Reggie said. "Even if he did, I wouldn't believe him. I mean, why shouldn't he act humble and sorry? He got his way. Max lost his job, and your father's turned against him. Hunter has his revenge. All he wants now is to get back with you."

"That's not true," said Anabelle, raising her voice, but she knew Reggie was right. She was suddenly tired, and felt more confused than ever. "Wait here," she whispered to Reggie. She hurried upstairs and brought back a letter she'd written for Max. "Could you take this to the hospital for me? Maybe it'll explain things better."

As she walked Reggie to the door, Anabelle could tell he was still annoyed.

"Are you getting back with Hunter?" he asked pointedly.

"You want an honest answer? I don't know. Just like I haven't decided about Max."

"Just tell me how you could even consider Hunter. He almost killed Max and hurt you—"

"That's over," she interrupted. Why couldn't Reggie see? "Hunter's not so bad. He and I go way back. He's done a lot of things for me. He looks after me. Puts up with my whims. I admit I sometimes went too far. I made him carry my kitten around the beach . . ."

Reggie looked puzzled for a moment. "What kitten?" he said.

"Muffin. I lost her a couple months ago. Hunter gave her to some girl to hold, and the girl never came back to the beach. Muffin was really cute, gold and brown stripes, a long tail."

Reggie backed off a moment, letting his thoughts collect. The cat he'd found on the beach was Anabelle's, had to be. He'd never forget the colors. The cat had been drowned—but how, or by whom? If Hunter was the last one to see it—Reggie knew that Hunter was crazy and cruel enough to drown a cat. Anabelle would make the connection, too. All Reggie had to do was tell the truth. She'd be hurt, but it would turn her against Hunter.

"What is it?" said Anabelle, sensing trouble.

Something burned in Reggie to let out the truth. He remembered the pizza incident, Hunter's merciless punches to his belly, the cold-blooded meanness of getting Max drunk and sending him out on the boat.

"Please tell me," Anabelle insisted.

"Tell you what?"

"What are you thinking?"

Go on, tell, thought Reggie. Anabelle thinks you're so honest . . . But after a moment he only shook his head.

"I'm not thinking anything," he said, after a moment, and tucking the letter to Max in a pocket, he headed out for some fresh air.

CHAPTER 27

Dear Max,

You probably think I'm totally rotten person for not taking your phone calls or coming to visit. I'm sorry if I hurt your feelings. The truth is I haven't forgotten you at all, because even if I tried it wouldn't be possible. You're bigger than life, Max. Are you feeling better? Is the food okay in the hospital? It must be boring sitting around all day, especially for someone as active as you. I hope your time isn't being spent wondering what I'm thinking.

Somehow I'll get this letter to you, which should explain my silence. The problem, my problem, is I have a terrible case of cold feet. I know that may sound silly and trite, but I'm suddenly afraid to make decisions about you and me. So much has happened so quickly this summer—I mean, you came on so strong—that only now am I starting to digest everything. This isn't meant to put you off, just to ask for your patience. Please know that I forgive you a hundred percent for what happened on the lake. Nothing was your fault.

Daddy may disagree, but it's our lives, isn't it? I think about you a lot. And miss you.
Please give me time to think.

Much love,

Anabelle

Reggie hovered near the bed. He hoped Max would share her letter. Max stared at the paper, transfixed, his eyes methodically rereading each line with the precision of a typewriter carriage. He finally lifted his glance to the window. Darkness had overtaken the town, leaving only twinkling lights in view.

"It's her father. He's the key," Max pronounced with new certainty. Reggie could almost hear a mental snap of the fingers. "Why didn't you bring me the letter sooner?"

"I had to be in my tower."

"You're too conscientious, anyone ever tell you that? Now give me that stationery over there . . ."

Max snaked his hand into the mammoth box of chocolates that Tiny had brought up earlier. Finishing one, he grabbed for another. "You're going to rot your teeth out," Reggie said as he fetched the writing paper.

"They give me energy," Max replied, smiling. "Good old energy."

"What are you going to write to her now?" Reggie inquired.

"Just that when I get out of this prison I want to meet with her father. I've got a new proposition. I'll work for free in any one of his stores, at least for a couple weeks. Just to make amends. To prove I'm an honest guy. How's that sound?"

"It sounds dumb," Reggie admitted as he paced the room. "No one's going to fall for that."

"But I'm serious! I'll work for nothing. You don't trust me?"

"It's too late for trust," said Reggie.

With an impish grin Max picked up a chocolate and hurled it at Reggie. "What's your problem today, fella?"

"My problem? My problem is I'm not going to deliver your letter. I'm tired of being a carrier pigeon."

"I don't believe this," Max exclaimed, throwing his hands up. "I ask you for one little favor and what happens? My good pal Reggie gives me lip."

"I'm sorry, but I don't want to see Anabelle anymore."

"Why? Something happening between you two?"

"Look," Reggie said, exasperated, "Anabelle's confused right now. She doesn't know what she wants. If you ask me, she's not going to get unconfused so fast, or worse, she's still hung up on Hunter. And I've gone to bat for you, Max, as much as I can. I can't do any more. Nor will your letters. Anabelle has to make up her own mind."

"You're wrong. The letters make a difference. They make Anabelle think about me. Reggie, I'm asking one last favor—"

"I've done you enough favors," Reggie shot back. He was tired of Max's pressure. And this whole routine was crazy. Whatever had to be said, Max could say it when he was released from the hospital. Besides, Reggie didn't want to see Anabelle anymore. He didn't want more questions about anything, including the cat. He didn't want to surrender to his dislike for Hunter and then end up hurting Anabelle. There'd been enough pain already. "I've paid you back for everything you've done for me," said Reggie. "And more. I pulled you from the lake—"

"So what am I supposed to do—bow down and give thanks?"

"For starters, yeah."

"How about a medal, too?"

"You just take everything for granted, you know that?" Reggie said accusingly. "You think things always are going to fall into place for you."

"They have so far."

"Like I'd be at the lake at the right time to save you? You almost expected it when you began to drown, didn't you?"

"Sure, you saved me," Max allowed. "I was lucky. I admit it. And I'm thankful. But jumping in that water and being a hero was something you did for yourself."

Reggie fell silent. He knew Max was right. The long, damp night had turned out to be a test of Reggie's own courage as much as anything else. But that wasn't the issue now. It was more than this favor or trust or friendship. The issue was Max's stubbornness, a blindness to reality. Why was he always knocking his head against a wall?

"What I'm trying to tell you," said Reggie, "for the zillionth time, is you're spinning your wheels. No matter how badly you want Anabelle, it's not going to happen."

Max flicked his hair from his eyes impatiently, as if he hadn't heard a word. "Reggie, all I'm asking you for is a little help. Till I'm back on my feet. Then I'll take care of everything."

"You make it sound simple."

"I need Anabelle," said Max.

Reggie studied Max for a moment, marveling at his determination, and even more than that, his optimism. He wasn't going to be denied, no matter how great the odds against him. One man against the world. Taking on all comers. Well, good luck, thought Reggie. As Max looked on imploringly, Reggie bowed his head and walked out of the room.

CHAPTER 28

Anabelle took a seat at the back of the ice cream parlor, studied the noon-time traffic of little kids, and waited for Reggie. She hoped that the note she'd given the bellhop at the Sherborne had found its way to the right cabin, because what she had to tell Reggie now was important. Anabelle rubbed her eyes, still tired. The sleepless night had been the longest in her life. So much to think about, important conflicts to resolve. She had been tempted to wake her parents and ask their advice, but that wasn't the answer. That was a cop out. What to do about Hunter and Max were her own problems, and *she* had to solve them. Her anxiety, her burden, was like an imaginary rock she carried around—a punishment for a summer of starting to take chances but not being mature enough to face the consequences.

This morning, up before her parents, she wasted no time. She woke Hunter at his house and, in a nervous voice, suggested he meet her to talk. "What's up?" he asked when they met. She thought Hunter could tell. Her heart hammered away, never at peace. The words came out thickly. "You'll always be special to me, Hunter. You were my first real boyfriend. But it's over for us. I feel now the same as I did at the start of summer, in spite of all that's happened. I want room to grow . . . to try new things."

She saw the shock and disbelief in his eyes, but there was nothing she could do about it, and it was a mistake to explain herself any further. Hunter would only try to talk her out of her decision. She gave him a good-bye kiss, then hurried on to the Sherborne, where she left the note for Reggie. The relief at having finished with Hunter was eclipsed by the anxiety of how to deal with Max. That's why she needed Reggie. He was a buffer, and though their encounter yesterday had been strained, she still liked and needed him.

Max was a problem. Maybe he'd always be one for her. In the last twenty-four hours she'd thought long and hard about their relationship. It wasn't her parents' feelings that had finally swayed her against Max; it was her own sense that while Max had helped her find herself this summer, she still had more discoveries to make. Max did too, even if he wouldn't admit it. What was difficult, and painful, was she still found him exciting. More than that, she really cared about him. The mind and what it resolved was one thing, but the heart had reasons all its own.

"Hi," she called, subdued, when she spotted Reggie in a T-shirt and shorts by the soda fountain. The sunburn on his legs had faded to a nice tan, she thought, and he'd put on a little weight. The arms were almost muscular. Reggie looked so different from the pale, uncertain boy she'd first met. He dropped into the seat across from her.

"You look beat," he observed."Are you okay?"

"Sure," she lied. She waited for her heart to slow down. "I guess there's no point in making speeches. You probably know why I asked you to come anyway." She wanted him to say "yes," to make it easier for her, but Reggie's face only furrowed in curiosity. "I won't be bothering you any more after today—"

"You don't bother me," he said sincerely. "If you mean yesterday, that's all right. I've forgotten it."

She tried to smile. "Today is rougher. I just told Hunter it's over for good."

Better to come right out and say it, she thought. Reggie looked relieved, or proud of Anabelle, as if he hoped all along she would make the right decision. "I guess you do what you have to," he said.

Anabelle's face suddenly flushed and she blinked back a tear. A damp handkerchief came out from her pocket. "I wanted to see you . . . so you could tell Max something." Reggie stiffened slightly, pushing back in his chair. "You have to tell Max that it's over for him and me, too."

Reggie shook his head uneasily. Maybe he felt as awkward as she did. "You knew this was coming, didn't you?" Anabelle asked.

He looked sad. "Yeah, I knew."

"Have you told Max what you thought?"

"Over and over. But he doesn't believe me. He won't believe me now, either. I think you'll have to tell him yourself."

"What do you mean?" She didn't understand. Why couldn't Max accept a "no?"

"He's crazy about you. He's in love."

"Please don't say that," Anabelle said.

"I have to say it. It's true."

Anabelle pressed her fingers against her temple, trying to compose herself. Things were moving out of control. "My decision has nothing to do with love. I'm just not ready for Max. When I was left in that boat, Reggie, I completely fell apart. What that showed me was I wasn't as grown up as I thought I was. It showed me I need more time to test myself. I want time to meet other people." She pulled back, looking at Reggie with hope. "Does that make sense?"

"It makes sense to me," Reggie admitted. "I hope Max will understand."

She sighed. Her hands were shaking. Why wasn't this working? Why couldn't Reggie be more helpful? "I don't think I can face Max. That's why I'm talking to you."

Reggie seemed frustrated. "I don't know what to tell you."

"Tell me I'm being fair. Say I'm not a villain. I'm not cruel. I don't want to hurt Max. I didn't just use him this summer—did I?" She dabbed the handkerchief to her eye again. "Sometimes I feel guilty—"

"You didn't use him," Reggie consoled her. "What you did, what you're doing now, happens to people all the time." He grabbed a breath, about to make a point. "But you have to see Max yourself. You owe that to him. After the way he chased you and everything."

She felt her face coloring. "It's too hard."

"You'll only hurt him more if you stay away. Just give him a reason. Tell him what you told me."

"I was counting on you to be a friend."

Reggie raised his hands in apology. "You'll have to come to the hospital. I mean, if you really don't want to be a villain . . ."

This was futile, she thought. Reggie was practically shaming her. What choice did she have? "Okay," she said. "I'll see him. Tomorrow morning. I'll come to the hospital."

She thanked Reggie for being a good listener, said good-bye, and headed outside. Had she done the smartest thing to make that promise? She owed Max a visit, and probably a lot more. The problem, and what she didn't tell Reggie, was she was totally afraid to confront Max. She was in fear of melting before him, renouncing her reasons for leaving him, falling under his spell again. Oh, Anabelle, she thought, you're a mess.

As she turned toward the shore road, a beach ball suddenly flew toward her, but at the last second she ducked, by instinct, and watched it skim harmlessly over the lake.

CHAPTER 29

"I don't believe you." Max struggled up in his hospital bed. The morning light filtered through the Venetian blinds in clearly defined bands. "What do you mean, Anabelle wants to break up?"

Reggie steeled himself for Max's outburst. He'd made a point with Anabelle that she give Max the bad news herself, but this morning he decided to warn his friend in advance. Max was so keyed up that to take the rejection cold would be disastrous. Now, at least, he had a chance to prepare for Anabelle's arrival.

"What did she say—*exactly?*" Max demanded.

"She didn't think it would work out because she wants more freedom."

"Who's boxing her in, anyway?" he asked. "Not me!" He jumped up and slipped on his robe, his arms flailing out wildly. "Who gave her that idea? You?"

"It was her own decision," Reggie said. "If it makes you feel any better, she dumped on Hunter, too."

Max propped a foot on his chair, looking bewildered. A nurse carried in his breakfast tray but he told her to set it on a side table. He was totally overwhelmed, Reggie realized. After a few moments Max began to pound a fist into his hand. Suddenly he laughed, at first nervously, then haughtily, as if Anabelle's rejection wasn't such a big problem after all. Reggie waited for a more desperate reaction, but when

Max turned around with his eyes and forehead set in concentration he said, "So she's kissing me off, huh?"

"I'm sorry," Reggie offered.

"But you said she promised to visit me. Right?" Reggie acknowledged it. "Then can't you see what's going on here, Reggie? This is nothing but a game. Another Anabelle Livingston game. I'm an authority on those."

"Max," Reggie declared, exasperated by his blindness, "I'm telling you she's serious!"

"Oh, she's serious all right. Serious for now. But when she sees me, everything will change. I guarantee it. I'll bet you the world. I've got a certain power over her." He gave Reggie a wink, as if this were some secret between only them. "When did she say she was coming?"

Reggie shrugged. "Some time this morning. Do you want me to leave?"

"What time is it now?"

"Twenty to nine."

"Stay," he ordered, and he ducked into the john. His hair was slicked back when he emerged, face cleanly shaven. He looked like his old self, Reggie thought. Physically dangerous and handsome, very much in control.

Reggie dropped into the chair and leafed through a sports magazine. He wanted to leave. He had a few minutes before he had to be in his tower, time to relax for a change, and he didn't want to be around when Max and Anabelle said their good-byes. The fireworks would be incredible. Max wanted him here, however, to witness what would be a royal battle of wills. "The trophy of victory will go to Max Riley," Max had predicted to Reggie. Reggie didn't doubt that Max was in love with Anabelle, deeply, but his ego was on the line too. "Hey, Reggie, haven't I always gotten what I wanted?" But as Reggie switched from one magazine to another, sneaking glances at his watch, he saw Max's confidence start to ebb. Max would rise from the bed, pace the room, make small talk, and stare longingly out the window.

"Where is she?" he finally said in frustration.

"I don't know."

"What time is it?"

"Five to twelve."

"Noon?" he said, shocked.

"Yeah."

"Then where the hell is she? What else is so important in her life? If she really wants to see me, why isn't she here?"

"Why are you getting so uptight?" Reggie said. "Anabelle is always late."

"No," Max said quietly, as if he sensed something that Reggie didn't. "She's not late and she couldn't have forgotten."

"What do you mean?"

"Let's go, pal. Quick—" He pushed his feet into his slippers and rushed toward the door.

"Where are we going?"

"Didn't you say Mrs. Livingston had packed Anabelle's bags for school?"

"Yeah, so? But that's for next week. Hey, you're not dressed—"

But Max was already gone. When Reggie caught up with him in the hallway, he pressed a finger to his lips, skulked past the nurses' station, and flew down a staircase and out a side door. Reggie darted after him. On the street Max started running as if on a desperate mission. Reggie grew winded as he tried to keep up. They cut through side streets and over lawns, blurring past white picket fences and Victorian mansions, moving up hills. Drivers stopped to gawk.

Max's bathrobe had come untied to float behind him like a cape. Superman, Reggie thought, only he couldn't fly.

But Max was fast on the ground. He looked like a halfback, head bent down, ready to break any tackle. Reggie worried that his lungs might still be weak, but Max showed no signs of faltering. They sprinted up a final hill, then rested on the crown as they gazed down on Anabelle's house. Her mother's station wagon was parked near the open front door, tailgate down. Reggie could make out Anabelle's steamer trunk inside. He was stunned, and sad for Anabelle.

Max suddenly threw back his head and gave a terrifying roar. He stormed toward the house. Reggie hurried after him, afraid for what might happen. Breathless, Max paused by the front door, and shouted for Anabelle. A figure emerged from the shadows of the hallway. Reggie watched uneasily as Mrs. Livingston blocked Max's path. Max pulled back for a moment, still glowering.

"Where's Anabelle?" he demanded.

"She's upstairs, but you can't see her." Mrs. Livingston's voice was calm but unyielding.

"I want to see her. I *have* to see her."

"I'm sorry, but that's not possible. Anabelle's been upset enough the last week. Right now I want to get her away from Barnswell."

"I have a right," Max insisted. He started to slip past her.

"If you still care about Anabelle next summer, you're welcome to see her then." Mrs. Livingston looked at Max coolly, with no hint of backing down. "I'd appreciate it if you would leave now. If you don't, I'll call my husband and he might call the police."

"Go call," he dared her. "I'm not leaving."

"Max—"

Anabelle's head peeked above her mother's shoulder. Reggie strained for a glance. She looked so lovely with her shiny hair falling just above her shoulders. Lipstick and makeup made her look mature. She wore a tweed suit.

"Mom, it's okay," Anabelle whispered. She looked at Max with a mixture of guilt and relief.

"Why didn't you come to the hospital?" he said, hurt, as she approached him.

"I wanted to, I really did. But at the last second . . ."

She dropped her head on his chest. Hesitantly, he let his arms wrap around her. "I guess I lost my nerve. Will you forgive me?" she asked.

"I don't want to forgive you. I want you to stay with me."

"I have to go back to school."

"Not right away."

"My parents want me to."

Max looked incredulous. "We're not talking about your parents! We're talking about you and me! I want you to forget your travel plans. Just for a couple days. I'll be out of the hospital. Hell, I'm out right now. We can spend all our time together."

"It's too late, Max."

"Too late for what? What are you talking about? It's just the beginning. Look at me, will you?"

She pulled back apologetically. "I have to go. Really. The train leaves in less than an hour."

"You're not listening!" Max's voice had become desperate. "I love you. I need you. I want to stay in Barnswell . . ."

"I love you, too. I think I always will." She circled her arms around his neck and kissed him consolingly. "Will you say good-bye to me now?"

"I'll never say good-bye."

She shook her head, fighting back a tear. "Please stop . . ."

"Anabelle, I'll do anything for you. You know that. Just give me another chance. One more chance to make good, that's all. Anything. Okay? Say it's all right."

"But it's not all right, Max. It never will be, and it's no one's fault."

"It *will* be fine, dammit. If you want it to be. Now come on, please . . ."

For a second she seemed willing to surrender. Her eyes half closed in pain. She looked like she wanted to say something. But then her face tightened. "No Max. It's over. I'm sorry I'm not the girl for you." She turned to the car. Her mother slipped behind the wheel, flicking the ignition key. The engine sputtered for an instant before coming to life. As Anabelle climbed in, Max watched, devastated, as if this scene couldn't really be happening. The car lurched forward with a painful certainty.

"No!" Max suddenly roared. The car eased out of the drive and rolled down the street. At first Max's legs moved slowly, tired from the run from the hospital, but then they picked up momentum. By the time he was in the street he was running for his life. It was Max's final gamble. Reggie didn't want to look.

For a few seconds Max closed in on the station wagon. He pushed an arm out, as if to stop it. His fingers scraped the back window. "Anabelle! Look at me!" When she didn't turn around, he shouted her name again. The car accelerated. "Anabelle!"

Max began to stumble. His right ankle gave way, and suddenly he was out of control, like some invisible hand was pushing him. He rolled over twice and fell against a curb. When Reggie got to him, his robe and pajamas were torn, his nose bloody. Reggie leaned over anxiously. "Max—"

"I'm okay," he answered after a moment, but his voice was shaky and he was slow pulling himself up. He was still trembling as his eyes jumped to the car, vanishing over a final hill.

CHAPTER 30

"It's too bad the summer ended the way it did," Reggie offered quietly as he nestled under a bushy pine tree. Max only grunted and tossed another rock into the lake, striking the moon's reflection dead center. The night air was turning colder but no one bothered to put on a sweater.

"You know, this is pretty much the spot where I was sitting the first time," Max admitted glumly. He touched the bandage on his nose to stop an itch. They'd finally discharged him from the hospital.

"The first time what?" said Reggie.

"That I saw Anabelle. She was skinny-dipping." The memory suddenly depressed him, and he tried to shake it off. "Reggie, do you ever play 'what-if'? Like, what if I had never seen Anabelle in the lake? What if she hadn't sat at my table that night? What if there'd never been a lifeguard strike? The summer would have been a lot different."

"You'll never know. It happened the way it happened. Anyhow, it's over."

"Yeah," he said moodily, but he didn't want to believe it.

Reggie popped open the last beer.

Max dropped a pine needle between his lips, letting it dance around like a toothpick. "You know, I've been thinking a lot about Hunter."

"What about him?"

"Even if he'd been the one to end up with Anabelle, he

wouldn't have been happy. No matter what he does with his life, he'll never be completely happy. He's too insecure. One day he'll own a Mercedes, but he'll want a Ferrari instead. He'll live in a gorgeous home, only he'll need a condo by the ocean, too. He'll marry a beautiful woman, and he won't trust her. He's his own worst enemy. I feel a little sorry for him."

"How do you feel about Anabelle?" Reggie ventured.

"Terrible."

"You can't pout forever."

"Maybe for just another hundred years."

"Sometimes you just have to let go, Max. You taught me that."

Max glanced over at Reggie. The way he had said it, Max realized Reggie was talking about his father. Reggie was looking ahead now. He'd come a long ways this summer, and Max was happy for him.

Max was still shocked that he'd lost Anabelle, just as he'd been incredulous that he couldn't swim to shore from the boat. But maybe he'd learned something about his limitations. In fact, his summer was pretty decent. The times with Anabelle had been very special. He was taking home a bundle of money—more than he'd anticipated making.

"What are you thinking?" asked Reggie.

"Just that you're right. It really is over." Max rose stiffly, gazing out at the lake. The image of the moon blurred just above that of the hotel, holding their wobbly shapes as if by magic. From his pocket Max pulled out a shiny brass key, cocked his arm, and catapulted it into the blackness. It made a quiet, forgotten ping as the water closed around it.

"Maybe we should get back to the cabin," Reggie suggested. "Tiny's planning a last-night party."

Max stopped him. "I'd like to say good-bye to you here.

After this, it's just going to be crazy." He extended a hand. Reggie took it reluctantly.

"I wasn't really planning on saying good-bye," Reggie said. "I wanted to keep in touch."

"Except for the letters to Anabelle, I'm a lousy correspondent."

"We could visit. I don't live that far from you. Maybe some weekend . . . And when I'm ready to buy real estate in California, I'll definitely come to you."

Max threw an arm around him, tugging playfully on his neck. "Reggie, you're all right. You're welcome anytime. Wait till you see my gorgeous mansion."

As they walked back to the cabin, Max pushed his tongue behind his teeth, and a sharp, carefree whistle split the air. He looked past the lights of Barnswell, pretending he could see into the night, a gift of sight that penetrated mountains and forests, that took him all the way to California.

What a summer, he thought. He had been so close to getting what he wanted. But he didn't want to think about that now. He'd just try again.

He could already imagine himself sitting behind the wheel of a sports car, wearing expensive clothes. Not a bad life. He'd feel right at home. Because if you believed in something enough, Max decided, you could make it come true.